It Cracks Like E

It Cracks Like Breaking Skin

STEPHEN FOSTER

faber and faber

First published in 1999
by Faber and Faber Limited
3 Queen Square London WC1N 3AU

Typeset by Faber and Faber Ltd
Printed in England by Clays Ltd, St Ives plc

© Stephen Foster, 1999

Stephen Foster is hereby identified as author
of this work in accordance with Section 77
of the Copyright, Designs and Patents Act 1988

'Walk Away Renee': words and music by Mike Brown/Bob Calilli/
Tony Sansone © 1966 Twin-Tone-Music Publ. Co. /assigned to Sunbeam-
Music Inc./assigned to Times Square Music Publications Co.,
Warner/Chappell Music Ltd, London W6 8BS,
reproduced by permisssion of IMP Ltd
'The Future', 'Everybody Knows' and 'Democracy' by Leonard Cohen,
reproduced by permission of Sony Music Entertainments

A CIP record for this book
is available from the British Library

ISBN 0–571–19506–7

2 4 6 8 10 9 7 5 3 1

for my family

Acknowledgements

Thanks for reading early drafts to : Elspeth Barker,
Marian Brandon, Marion Catlin, Jack FF, Marion Forsyth,
Andrew Motion, Andrew Smith and John Street.
Special thanks to Julian Loose at Faber and to
George Szirtes at Norwich School of Art and Design.
Extra special thanks to David Hill, who I was
alongside at UEA.

Contents

It Cracks Like Breaking Skin

Big Wheel

Sad sweet dreamer, it's just one of those things you put down to experience. Oohhwahhwahh.

SoulMusic rides on the dusk, on candyfloss. New landscaped ground falls away, brown smoked, marked by two cinder orange paths, one for bikes, one for people. A rule that no one obeys. The grass is spare and the thin trees are ringed by wire netting. The strip is long and broadens to a low plateau at the bottom. The pithead gears lean against the sky. The Big Wheel turns. Where did the funfair pitch up before the landscaping, when it was just a bank of black ash? Don't know.

It's dangerous to go down there on your own. There are gangs of HeathEnders and Banksiders. They lurk around the edges of the rides and stalls. They nick the boy's money, then they beat him up. If he can avoid this, get inside without it happening, it's safer though, because there are plenty of grown-ups he can pretend to be with. What he has to do is keep cover as much as he can – wriggling on his belly is best – and wait for the gap when someone else is getting beaten up.

Cuts in through the queue for the Helter Skelter.

The first person he sees is Robert Gilligham, Nigel

Gilligham's brother. Rob leans against the railing at the Waltzer's edge. The spinning backs of the cars reflect in his glasses, his head seems to be fazing in and out with them. The cars are turning so fast you can't even tell who's in them, the people all blur into one. Rob is watching the man who's whipping the riders. Bet he's wondering how those men stay standing up like that, managing even to walk on the track between the cars. It seems impossible. That's what the boy's wondering Anyway. He doesn't want to talk to Gilligham, so he moves round the warm engine of a hot-doughnut van and up a step into the arcade. The planked floor sounds hollow under his feet. The man in the booth exchanges five twos for a ten, twenty-five for a fifty – he has the monies stacked up in equal piles. The boy should check his change all the same, just to be on the safe side. On a Thursday and Friday between half-six and half-eight, the boy collects the Pools with his mum. He gets paid. He has to be careful with the actual Pools money. Just two lines this week, Duck, they say, if they're not doing their usual, if they're saving or something. It's then that he needs to be careful, because he knows the amount they normally do so he has the exact right change ready in his hand, and he has to sort it all out again. It's a nuisance. And if he gets it wrong – and he has to do the sum in his head on the spot – people can think he's changing them short. He wouldn't anyway, because he'll see them next week, and every week, but they still Might Think. Funfairs, though, they're here today gone tomorrow, so best watch out.

He drops some coins into the PennyFalls. The money all looks nice laid out flat and shining, but winning is hard. Most often you can get out about the same as you put in. If you're lucky. You've got a better chance than on the Donkey Derby anyway.

Girls work behind the kiosks. Glamour Girls, DollyBirds. Always chewing. In one kiosk the girls pass over the hooks to fish for the ducks with numbers on the bottom, in another they hand out the rifles to shoot at the ducks that go along on a target. He doesn't know what ducks have ever done to deserve it. One glamour girl walks round the inside of the circle calling, Test Your Skill, Three Darts A Go. They're not properly weighted, his dad says. His dad says they don't stick. Every One A Winner, the sign says. A man with his girlfriend resting in on him laughs and licks the tips of the arrows, like it's some kind of magic secret, but before the boy sees the man throw he has to hide down quick. From a HeathEnder coming his way, a HeathEnder with a raised brown mole on one cheek, like a pimple, who Always wants to beat the boy up. The boy's Always running from him. The BrownMole's got a few others with him as well. The boy's heart starts beating, and his knuckles scrape the dust. He waits a bit before rising, peeping slow over the counter to see if BrownMole is still there. He can't see him, but he's sure he won't have gone. The third dart flights in overhead. The man's stuck three cards! Chooses a cuddly dog from the middle shelf. A present for his girl-friend. Wow.

One of the Pools customers is an invalid woman. Her house is set a little away from those in the rest of the

5

round, down a lane. The boy runs to do her while his mum picks up a few down a cul-de-sac. There's a gate at the side, he has to lean over to undo the latch. He goes in through the back because the woman can't answer the front door. He goes in through a little conservatory lean-to which has a funny smell. There's a different funny smell in the kitchen, where she sits, in her chair. It's like a rocking chair but she doesn't move in it. She sits by the side window.

Oh hello, love, is it you? she always says. What have you got to tell me?

Nothing much, he usually says back. He's in a hurry Actually, but he doesn't show it.

'Is your school alright? Are you doing well?'

Got a BPlus for me English, he tells her. He tells her he played for the football team Tuesday after school, that they won two-nil, beat Stanfields, but that he didn't score. He was only sub, to be honest. And he starts backing out.

Bye, love, she says. Fingers crossed, eh?

They all say that.

Cuts through an entry to catch up with his mum in the next street.

The girlfriend crooks the cuddly dog against her side, the man lays his arm across her shoulder, the boy follows close behind. Like these are the ones he's with. They move over to the Dodgems. They just miss the ride, so they all stand, standing and watching. The start-up whrrr of the cars together with the tannoy voice and the soundtrack music overhead out of the speakers all crackles: All Fares One Way One Way Round the Track You to me are everything the sweetest song that I can sing oh baby One Way Now All Riders.

Bumping heads jolt back bumped.

Blue sparks from the silver stems.

Now he runskids across the floor. He's after the orange car, the fast one. It's Always the orange one that's the fast one. You have to be quick to get the one you want, you know. Another man just like the spinner one on the Waltzer slides round taking the money. Have the right change ready, don't give 'em a note. The dodgems man rides on the back of cars that have girls in them, or he gets children unstuck when they're wedged in at the side or trapped in a ruck they can't get out of. Boys don't want him on the car. The man knows that. If he steps onto a boys' car, it's to piss them off. Ride On. The boy swerves and rolls, foot flapping the steel pedal, arm over the wheel like you do, one-handed steering out of danger. Apart from when he rams straight into the side of the man with the girlfriend accidentally-on-purpose. Some people call them bumping cars, some people call them dodgems. When the ride's nearly over, he spots Brown-Mole, Again, standing at the edge of the track by the steps. Shit. Shit. He can try to pull up at the other side, it'll give him a start, but not much. Maybe BrownMole's just waiting for a go for himself. Perhaps he hasn't noticed the boy, Even.

When the boy and his mum finish the round they drive over to Tunstall, take all the coupons and all the money to a house at the top end near Furlong Road. All the collectors take their calls there, two blokes sit at a big table, stacking the monies in equal piles. They make sure it all matches and tallies before the boy and his mum can go. (It's only his mum who Really has to stay.) The collectors tell each other stories, who wasn't in and what have you, how some people never remember to do it, always the same ones you have to call back on. (Those are the ones the boy gets sent back for Actually.) It's quite boring for him, the talking, so he often leaves early, walks home. There's a park on the way and he sometimes plays on the swings, his wages shifting in his pocket, rolling against his thigh, chinking. He walks up Little Chell towards home. One night, he sees BrownMole coming down the other side of the road, and he slips into the drive of his mum's aunt's family's house. They don't know him well really, and when he knocks they aren't in anyway. They've got swings in the back garden on the lawn. It's always mown. They've got a shed too. He hides round the back of the shed. BrownMole saw him. The boy hears BrownMole's steps on the drive and has to climb over the back fence – there's a gap there between the houses that you can squeeze through. He tears his trousers and scrapes his hands on the thorns.

The boy pushes out of the car, swinging from the pole and jumps off the track. BrownMole is wearing the look of death, coming round the one side, running. His mates are coming from the other side. He's definitely definitely seen the boy. Pelterfuckingskelter. Double-dead-lucky: the boy clatters straight into Janice Stevens. HeyUp Duck, she says, You're in a hurry. She's Stevens's older sister. She goes to work. Stevens is in his class at school. There's another sister called Dionne. She works too. On a FridayNight sometimes, after the pools, the boy and Stevens hang about, talking, while the sisters get ready to go out. They take hours in the bathroom, one gets in first and locks the door, but they end up having to share it, and the door stays open. They push each other about in front of the mirror. They argue, but they don't mean it. There's perfume and all that everywhere and their hair lacquer makes you choke. They always leave together, Janice and Dionne, down the steps to the street, linked. Stevens doesn't pay all that much attention Actually, he isn't bothered, he checks the telly page to see what's on the late-night horror. It's the boy who's interested in see- ing how it all works because he hasn't got older sisters. The girls do notice. They play records all the time they're getting ready and they dance: Now that we've caressed, a kiss so warm and tender, I can't wait till we reach that sweet moment of surrender. They play that one a lot. Over and over.

As Janice speaks to the boy, BrownMole pulls up short and his gang check in behind.

I'm going on the Big Wheel, she says. Do you want to come? I'll pay you on.

Yeah, Thanks. Yeah.

When the wheel rolls over the top, he can see all the way to the houses where they collect the pools. He can see the chimney of the house where the invalid woman lives. He think it's that one anyway. One FridayNight she said that her grandson was in the front room, and called through.

'Come and see the boy who collects the coupon. The one I was telling you about.'

Nothing happened.

'Come on, get yourself away from that telly.'

Nothing happened.

She smiled at the boy, saying, He does dawdle. I don't know how he ever gets to school on time.

The grandson came through.

'What've you got your shoes on for? Why did you take off your slippers?'

Nothing.

'You don't know each other then?'

They shook their heads. This was the first time the boy had seen BrownMole. He's not a bad lad, she said to the boy, nodding at BrownMole. When he remembers to be. He does some shopping for me in the week, don't you? This was the first time the boy had seen the look of death.

BrownMole said nothing and moved back into the front-room.

The thing about a Big Wheel ride when it ends is you're still on it for ages, unless you're the first off or nearly. The boy and Janice finish up just past the platform, so they get to go round again. They don't mind.

'I can see our house, over there, see, next to the grass. Can you see yours?'

He can't Actually.

They jerk towards the top.

'Look, there's our Dionne, by the waltzer.'

The boy can't pick her out. He's leaning over to see if They've Gone.

Who is it you're looking at? Janice says.

Some boys. They want to get me.

'Why?'

I don't know. I think it's . . . I don't know.

When they come to get off, Janice says, It's great, the fair. Don't you love it? Have you had a toffee apple?

No.

'We'll get a couple then, shall we?'

Yeah, Please. Yeah.

When they climb out of the chair, the man who lifts the guard rail says something to Janice which she ignores. Janice links the boy's arm and Dionne checks in and links up on the other side, shows Janice a charm that the Waltzer-spinner man gave her. Janice makes a face. BrownMole seems to have gone missing. The boy sees Robert Gilligham scrabbling between legs, trying to save a goldfish. The boy stands ahead of Janice and Dionne in the toffee-apple queue as Janice lays her hands over his shoulders, holding him to her, swaying gently to the SoulMusic riding on the dusk. The shadow of the Big Wheel rolls across the ground. The pithead gears lean against the sky.

Life on Earth

On the ground and around, the closer the tighter and the more compact, the houses' front doors step straight onto the pavement and in between the shops do the food and the ciggies and the papers. Some shut early on MatchDays. Grilles up. Metal grilles. Smell the onions and the sweat, the mild the bitter the black and tan, meat and potato, steak and kidney, burger, sausage, gravy-seeping newsprint warm soggy and hot like only gravy-seeping newsprint. Not like anything else. Crooked, man in a doorway, flame, lighting pipe. Roll-up, Embassy, fat cigar. Camel-hair car coat. Sheepskin jacket. Salt, vinegar, ketchup, the holy trinity. Thermos flask sticking out of a pocket. Tartan pattern.

Legs swinging from a crush barrier. Silk scarves tied to our wrists. Rock hard.

If you were a bird and looked down right now, movement would be all towards one place. Tributaries linking and flowing, coming in from all ends, our ends and the other ends, moving and shaking, snaking and faking, people of the world everybody join hands like a love train, rocking, rolling, clocking, strolling, ducking and diving. But you wouldn't see that from up there, not the ducking and the diving.

And the louder the rhythm, the stamping and the stomping and the shoving pushing darting rucking and mauling. Stops. It stops. Us and them us and them us and them. Sudden. Dead. How does it stop like that? Two lines torn, broken in formation. A stand-off. Alsatian stretching at its leash, unglued jaw snarling, and another one, identical, only feet away inexplicably sitting quiet to attention like a statue at the gate of a big house. The undercarriage of a horse, black and tan with swinging balls. There on the concrete, steaming, a mound, brown sugar straw manure. And the horse rearing, forelegs in the air.

Whoah there whoah boy. Whoah whoah whoah. Calmdown.

Dead silence.

The sound of two hands clapping. The sound of four hands clapping. The sound of eight hands clapping, twelve hands clapping. Horn. Horn. Horn horn horn . . .

FarFarFarFar ¡CITY!

How does it start, that?

Legs swinging from a crush barrier.

Never seen any one single person start it you know. But once, clicked through the turnstile early, up OurEnd, right at the very front of the back, pole position, saw a guy with a knuckleduster. Watched him put it on. Four fat rings, like plumbing, glinting, welded round his fingers. Unglued jaw snarling skinhead. A six-footer. Spurs. Saw that. Saw that start. Saw him start it. The mob circling.

◆

13

C'mon then, C'mon, C'mon, C'mon then. Y'Cunt. I'll ave ya.
C'mon. I'll ave ya. C'mon. Cunt. Kin Cunt.

Cauldron. Cunt, farking cunt. Heard that. Underneath it all, us. Too small, too small, too small. Actually, you don't lean down to use a knuckleduster you know. Smash upwards, all the way to Heaven. Follow through. Maximum impact. How would that look like from up there, from way up high, what would it look like? Say you were in a helicopter, looking out looking through a telescope. Dew kicked off a flower-head in the early morning dawn. Like that, only red. Showered in it, we were. Not for the first time neither.

Legs swinging from a crush barrier.
  Programme! Programme! Golden Goal! Golden Goal!
  See these guys, they get to watch the game for free. That's why they do it. Cos you wouldn't want to do it, rucks rolling by, kicking the stand over, you know, the stand with the programme or the golden goal on it. You wouldn't want to do it.
  Nobody ever wins golden goal. It's impossible Anyway.
  Kick the fucker over, fucker, kick the fucker over.
  Rucks rolling by. Legs swinging from a crush barrier.

Not the first time neither. A body came passed over our heads when we were down at the front one time, right behind the posts, where you can shout to the keeper. Knifed. Knifed in the neck. Didn't get any on us that time, it wasn't really flowing though, not like against Spurs.

14

Wolves that was. Gold scarf tied round his wrist. Rock hard. Take OurEnd, that's what they try. NoWay. No Fucking Way. St John's took hold of him, pulled him onto the track over the hoardings. Laid out flat on a stretcher on the ground. Hospital job. Cheered off.

After. Tight tight squeeze, you get carried out, feet off the ground, mashed between the bodies.

One time all the away end left at once, four-nil down they were, twenty minutes to go. Outside, broke every window in sight.

After, there's just the halo-glow of the floodlight, dark and mist. On the way to the station, we hurdle tombstones in the graveyard just nearby, terrified, Burnley or West Ham trying to kill us. We're not too small to chase, too small to chase too small to chase. Not for that. We're fucking fast though. We've got the jumps. We know the route you see. We Know the score. If we're lucky, one of them twists an ankle or breaks a leg, sliding and writhing over the marble slab hidden in the grass. Catch us if you can. Fuckers. Catch us if you can. Across the road and through that foyer, mosaic floor, cold, hard, marked-out with a big star shape, skid across and onto the train, clatter through the doors.

Whoah. Watch it there, young un. Steady.

Police and guards everywhere.

Safe.

How'd City get on then?

Same old man, every week, Always asks that. How can anyone not Know the score by now. How?

◆

15

Legs swinging from a crush barrier. You won't believe it, but when it's quiet and only us there, early, before the gates even open, we do gymnastics on those barriers. The vaulting horse, beam, parallel bars. Olga Korbut. Champions we are.

It Cracks Like Breaking Skin

Purple face and smell of last night's beer still too fresh, Frank drives, and with fayther in there beside him pulls up sharp. Watch them through the streaking window; see my day begin. Shivering youth in anorak wrapped up double warm but cold still I climb into door round wet side of van.

'Aye up, youth, at awreight?'

The two faces turn and shine in greasiness and they wear a family resemblance unchanged as each bears the same stamp but oddly it's the younger one looks older. He's in charge, and while I think about it now, maybe he felt it a burden. The younger one looks as though no woman ever cared for him save his mother who gave that up a long time ago. The younger one is fat and wears a clean white overcoat like a mackintosh, dirty slacks and brown leather boots with elasticated sides. I give him a look, a negative reply to the question of greeting. I'm not awreight. It's too early too be awreight. It's still dark.

'As she bin lying on it again, youth?'

I try a half smile. My imaginary girlfriend lying on my imaginarily lengthy dick making the morning a hard one to get up on. Fayther cackles at this.

'If they dusner know how to look after her, they can allus send her to may young un, they knowest.'

He bangs his elbow into my side. I like Tommy more than Frank, so I make a bigger effort at a smile. But it's more of a grimace as face muscles won't do a smile, not yet.

How many imaginary girlfriends is this? Are we all sharing the same one or have we got one each? I think about it as we roll past the Methodist Hall where I used to sing hymns when I was young, as we splash through the puddle at the bottom of the hill where the road won't drain. Grey water laps at the skirts and the motion makes a rollocue as through the window the park passes by in black and grey and the railing tops faze like whipped sparklers on bonfire night because all the spikes are in gold and municipally well-kept and I want to go back to sleep but Frank farts, loud, long and noxious, and Frank laughs.

The van turns left and right and right and glides up a little brow and flattens off at the top and there we are by the market doors.

The first. We're always the first. Van doors open and close with thin metal clunks and I put on a white overcoat too, I pull it on over everything, anorak and jumpers, the works, for this bit. Tailgate rises slow and inside carcasses swing gently, the motion not yet stopped in them. Frank takes the big cuts, quartered cows, I take halved ewes, lighter; Tommy takes metal trays, like bread crates, the higher ones dry with sausage and eggs, the low ones seeping blood from black shining livers which lap around as he carries them.

We take the carcasses through double doors, one long walk to the right, another to the left delivers us to a slab of marble in the middle of the ultimate aisle. Above the marble glides a rail in chrome and shines and from it hang hooks, naked now but soon to be furnished with knuckles and best-ends.

'Cans't get tea, fayther?'

Fayther makes tea. I begin to take a side of mutton apart on the left-hand chopping block, a little lower than the one Frank works at beside me. We face the back of the stall as we dismember, cold ceramic wall, fat and blood smeared, we hang the cuts up above and to the side of us, and we pull them down again for finer dissection, ribs becoming chops or crowns or eyes.

Eye of lamb, love, seventy pence a pound.

Mutton to lamb, woman to love. Women always buy, men hang back, wanting to be somewhere else, not knowing about meat or buying, only knowing it's to be on the table at the right time on Sunday or else. That's what they say, anyway.

On the floor two cardboard boxes collect the bones and the fat. Fayther looks after these. His own little business on the side. Bones for the dog, fat for basting. Free of charge to special people, those with something to offer, a hug or a kiss, or a nod, a wink, a shared drag, a tip.

My hands are freezing. I warm them up in a bucket of water that was hot three-quarters of an hour ago. It's only lukewarm now so it takes longer. As I lean to get my hands into the bucket, everything goes black. I straighten up seeing stars. Black stars. Frank, seeing me pale, shows concern.

'More tea for the lad, fayther. Plenty of sugar.'

In the corner is a walk-in cold store which all the butchers use. The whole of this aisle is butchers' stalls. We need more lamb. Passing by Smith's as they pile up the pork pies, arrange the slices of ham and tongue, hang the bunches of gleaming black puddings and sausages, decant the moulds of brawn, on the corner there I pass a handbag stall, not yet open, and into the fridge. Fuck. Cold. Fuck. Don't waste time in here and worry too – if door closes behind, locked in till someone notices, the hum of freezing and only the rigored corpses for company. Hoist a side of lamb onto my shoulder and walk out, upright as possible. Nonchalant. Big tough guy. Hook it up on rail and Tommy assists.

'Aye up, youth. Thay't getting strong awreight.'

From the double doors over to the left an old woman appears. Maybe she's not that old. She looks old. She stoops in her walk. She has thin, matty hair, wears a coat all threadbare, scrawny legs hang out beneath, disappear into plastic boots. The first customer of the day. I look over to the clock at the back of Forester's stall. Five to eight. It's my job to serve this woman. Frank doesn't like her. She doesn't pay well. She'll ask me to weigh the cheapest cut we have, neck of lamb, and when I give her the price, she'll look at me imploringly, as if this is too much, forty pence or some such, like I could do a reduction on it. I've had to learn to be hard, you know. All the same, I can't catch her in the eye while we go through the routine. Frank does his bit.

'Come on, lad, they'st cutting-up to do back here they knowest.'

That's right, chivvy things along with your back to me Frank, braveman. The needle on the scale rocks slowly, settling on one pound fourteen ounces. We can both read it, me and the woman, scales read from both sides. Still it's forty pence.

Sorry, that's the best I can do, I say.

She smiles. They say watery, don't they? She smiles watery, wet with a couple of tears.

Alright, darling, she says, I know you do your best for me.

I slip my overcoat off and pull on my striped apron as I watch her move off round the corner towards the fruit and veg stalls.

'Looking for something for nothing.'

Frank brings a cleaver down onto the block. 'They're all the same.'

Jesus.

Frank's friend Don has the end stall. Don has a glass eye. It's hard to tell where he's looking. Don's daughter Cheryl who works there on the stall with him is tall and gawky, and often in tears, I don't know why. She has a good body. A reight good body. I should give a fiver to smell one of her farts, youth, Frank says. I swivel my eyes up to heaven, honest I do. There's a glass roof there, all wrapped in wrought iron, steep pitched, way up high. Sun streams through on good days and lights up the dust. I tilt my head back and I roll away.

'What say, youth? Woulds't like to get they hands on her, ey?'

No, I reply, and I dig the point of the knife into a sheep's shoulder, start to tease out the blade bone.

Don has a wife who also works on the stall with him. She's a little, round battleaxe thing. She and Frank pretend to like each other, but they don't.

Two of my favourite customers arrive. A mother and daughter combination. The mother is at the stall-front, making decisions on the week's meat, the daughter pulls up just behind. She has long brown hair, wavy, and a gap between her front two teeth. She has large black eyes and pale skin. She's wearing a corduroy three-quarter-length coat in dusky blue. Because we're at the same school, she refuses to look me in the eye. I serve her mother a three-pound piece of silverside and some liver. I'm so polite.

Yes, of course, some fat, sure, there you are, yes, no trouble, thank you; isn't it? – for the time of year. Bye.

I'm in love with the daughter girl of course. We never speak.

As they move off, the mother's voice carries through the air saying, That Hewitt lad from your school, he's a polite boy. He's got good manners, hasn't he?

The daughter girl says nothing.

Joan arrived about two hours ago. Joan does Saturdays. Me, Frank and Joan are crammed behind the stall, serving and cutting furiously. Tommy's to the side, smoking. It's elevenish now, the heat of the morning. Shop, lad, shop, urges Frank if it appears that I'm slacking for even a second. It's imperative to get customers served, keep them from straying off to rival stalls.

'Shop, youth, shop.'

Shut up Frank you fat git. Not out loud.

Frank bends down. Under the counter there's a dandelion and burdock pop bottle which Tommy brought back from the Sneyd Arms fifteen minutes ago, filled with mild ale. He takes a swig and straightens up. Cheered, he turns to do a little serving himself. At this time of day, alcohol fumes are easy to pick up, being relatively rare yet. No one seems bothered.

I get out from behind the stall, give myself fifteen minutes off for a cruise round. Next aisle, study a pile of cheeses, the stench from which wafts my way all day. They appear odd, these cheeses, I can't quite make them make sense. They don't seem like food somehow. The stallholder looks like a cheese himself, round-packed and fat. Across from here, two fruit stalls, apples and oranges arranged in pyramids which you long to have a shy at. Sometimes they do tumble of their own accord, juicing the pavement underfoot. Beside the fruit stalls, a fabric stand run by a woman in a crochet top with a full face on. She always smiles. Turn corner, remove apron.

Down at the end, a long corner site sells sweets and biscuits, belongs to an elderly couple and their niece helps out on Saturday. Lynne. And Lynne is so beautiful but way way beyond me because Lynne is older and speaks well and has perfect skin and perfect haircut, lips with gloss and works in the clean without blood or dirt or smell but with the glitter of a thousand sweets. Lynne doesn't notice me yet. Good. And edge around the corner before she does so I can come back later and she'll think it's the first time today.

Put apron back on and squeeze through the crowds, bumping shopping trolleys and wicker bags, over to the far corner for tea and oatcake rolled up, soft, dripping with melted cheese. Sit up high on a bar stool and watch women behind counter, all plump and wearing hairdos, striped overalls and glasses, glasses all steamed up by the urn, working like a dance, working with tea, working with toast and butter or dripping, and scones with or without. Everybody drinking from a cracked cup. Working like a dance.

Back on the stall.

'Eye up, lad. Wheres't bin?'

Say nothing but give everyone a scone instead.

'E's a good lad, in't he?'

Being a good lad's not hard round here. Feed people. That's how.

Later, when I've scrubbed the blocks down with sawdust and a brush made of thick wire filaments which pull the blood and fat out of the grain, scoured the marble, slooshed the trays, swept the concrete. Later, on the bus home, a bag safe between my feet. For my mum, full of joints and sausages, chops and liver, bacon and eggs. Later. Later I break a kidney out of its fat, feel it tear and yield the shiny organ to my hand, like a jewel. Then I do it again. I've got lots. I've been collecting kidneys today like conkers in September. When you tear the fat, it cracks like breaking skin. Back home, I cook. He's a good lad.

Frank tosses me some ribs to chop up. Tommy screws a cigarette into his mouth and lifts bones from the box, wraps them in newspaper, presses them into the arms of one of his chunky paramours. Cheryl passes by on a return from the fridge, Frank winks at her and she begins to look tearful. Joan's son turns up and with him his fiancée, permed and hazed. Joan does them a brisket at a good price. Frank leans down and swigs from the bottle. In my mind's eye I have a vision of blackcurrant and liquorice sweets, wrapped in purple shining paper, twisted and bowed.

Fall

Several years later, on the top deck of a bus, cigarette smoke licking at the condensation on the panes, Hewitt overheard two apprentices behind him discussing what had become of their former classmates. Finimore, they said, was working with his dad, fitting carpets. It was alright, they said, the money was good, but his knees would be fucked by the time he was forty. Hewitt drew a square on the window and watched the water trickle off its bottom corners to collect in a pool at the lower edge of the frame.

Hewitt hadn't known Finimore well. Finimore had been in the same year but several classes below him and as such was one of the hard men. The Law of School – bright, therefore weak, or not bright, therefore strong. Finimore was one of those boys who developed man parts before his time. When he was fifteen he was six feet tall with facial hair and a heavy body odour that he left behind him in the corridor after he had passed by. He wore a leather jacket, had a swagger as wide as the road and was widely reckoned not a virgin. He was a fighter, but the kind that needed to be provoked rather than the psychotic antagonist type. Hewitt was not a coward, but was of only regular size and disliked physical pain. He got along by keeping his head down. A bully named Wilkinson once picked a fight with him beside the dinner hall at the end of the day. Hewitt was unaware of the reason for this, but there didn't necessarily have to be one. There was a scuffle of punches and a quick gathering of a crowd in the normal way. He'd lost, but not as heavily as the audience were expecting, though it could have been worse had the approach of a couple of teachers not cut it short.

Wilkinson. Hewitt could picture him now, ill-dressed and ugly. Two days later, after the story had gone round, Hewitt heard that Finimore and his mates had given him a pasting outside the bottom gates. He didn't know whether this was connected with his fight, but he knew that it meant Wilkinson wouldn't try it on again too soon, just in case, and so felt protected. The protection spread wider than against Wilkinson alone, because others were not sure whether Finimore's actions implied that a pasting could be issued to anyone who tried Hewitt for a fight. He felt residual gratitude toward Finimore in the knowledge of this, and although they never exchanged words, he felt confident enough to offer him the occasional nod of greeting together with an accompanying grunt, which he found reciprocated in a diminished but none the less discernible reply.

A few months after the Wilkinson incident, Hewitt found himself in the company of Finimore and assorted boys from their year in the school minibus. They were to deliver parcels of food to old people at the nearby houses and on the estates, part of the harvest festival. The day was clean, crisp, blue-skied autumn. Fall, the Americans called it. Hewitt had learned this in English Lit and liked the description very much.

We're in the season of Fall, Stevens, he drawled transatlantically to his friend as he fell in beside him on the walk to school, continuing, The Americans call it Fall because that's when the leaves depart the trees, see? He kicked up a large drift.

These are the Fallers, you see. It's kinda obvious.

He checked sidelong. Stevens was unmoved.

Colored like copper and bronze, Man. Hewitt stretched his accent wider.

'Have you done your Chemistry homework? By the way, your accent's crap.'

See You Jimmy. Hewitt switched to a Glaswegian growl and stuck his neck out in unconvincing aggression.

'Well done, Hewitt.'

Well done what? Hewitt reverted to his usual voice, defined by a permanent faint incredulity.

'Cu. Periodic Table. Chemical symbol for copper. Very good.'

Stevens was a smart chap. No doubt about it. He'd go far.

Hewitt and Stevens had been selected for the minibus trip because they had a specialized skill. They could use the school darkroom, and so were nominated official photographers for the outing. The school darkroom was a well-kept secret. It was only by persistent nagging of the Art teacher, after class when no one else could overhear and interlope, that he and Stevens had managed to gain access to and tuition in the secrets of this space. They needn't have worried about the others. When they were discovered one dinner time by several of their classmates emerging from a door previously supposed to be a store-room, they found themselves subject to charges of homo-sexuality. Two boys spending time together in a dark room is absolute confirmation of perversion. Hewitt and Stevens, though, were far too seduced by the alchemic process, the magic paper, the dim red light, the chemical vapours, and so accepted that they'd have to accept the taunts.

The minibus swinging out of the school gates was driven by Mr Best. Besty, as he was known, but the softening of his name held no implication of affection. Besty had arrived at the school as Deputy Head and had instigated a previously absent regime of unpleasant discipline. The actual Head, Boris the Bold, was a big ginger man whose position seemed to be largely honorary. He was a figure of fun. Besty was military: clipped moustache, defined jaw, strong neck, trim, clean and hard. His eyes were a dead cobalt. He dealt out a lot of punishment and enjoyed it. Hewitt had the cane from him once, a single blow to each hand. It hurt less than he was expecting, but Hewitt had only been in his third week at the school, up for his first offence, and the severity of the stroke reflected that. Prior to the punishment, he and two other boys also appearing on the same charge stood in line in Besty's office. Deputy Best began by displaying his armoury to them, describing the type of offence and the age of offender to which each implement was appropriate. They ranged from standard canes to a flat, whippy piece of timber shaped like a cricket bat that was used for bigger boys, administered to the arse in multiples of six, they learned. At the conclusion of the description of each weapon, Best brought it cracking down onto the desk for effect. What Hewitt had most disliked was the humiliation of the standing wait while this exhibition took place. He was frightened alright, but he was aware of the pleasure Best was getting from it and it made him feel sick. He was never whipped again.

But there were boys who were up in front of Best often. Everyone knew who they were. Finimore was one of these. During an unusual event like the harvest delivery, normal attitudes were relaxed, there was a slight air of off-duty. Hewitt noticed that Best behaved with Finimore like an edgy father with an errant child. There existed between them an understanding that Finimore would be treated like a regular human being so long as he avoided transgressing any of Best's Laws.

The minibus parked up at various spots, and cardboard boxes containing tins of plum tomatoes, jars of sandwich spread, packet soups and so on were distributed to addresses nearby. Shredded paper was used as packing. The parcels were called Hampers. The old people had been nominated by school-goers who had identified them as exceptionally poor, which seemed to mean exceptionally old. Hewitt and Stevens accompanied one giver or more each time they stopped and photographed the delighted recipients as it became clear to them what was going on. Most of them seemed pretty impressed, and Hewitt and Stevens were enjoying the gift of giving almost as much as their new status as skilled artists. Best got into several shots, creepily displaying his largesse for the benefit of the camera. The photographs would be displayed on a board at the front of the special harvest assembly in two days' time.

Towards the end of the morning, with almost all the Hampers delivered, Finimore called Hewitt down a back alley.

Do you want a drag? he asked, offering Hewitt a pull on a cigarette.

Hewitt did smoke. Among other things, it improved his standing with the hard men. But Hewitt had the edge on common sense that Finimore so obviously lacked.

He refused, with the line, It's a bit early for me.

Mixed feelings. The offer constituted an overture of friendship on Finimore's part. Hewitt shuffled a pile of leaves, balancing a few loose ones on his shoes, tried another: It's good to be out of school, isn't it?

'Aren't fucking bothered. Be out soon enough in any case.' Finimore ground the fag under his toe. 'T's get back before that bastard Best catches us.'

Yeah, Hewitt replied, finishing the awkward exchange by turning his attention to messing with the camera.

Back in the minibus. Finimore sat in the front, as Best had instructed, the unoccupied centre seat allowing him to be one space away. In the back, Hewitt unloaded the film, kicking Stevens on the ankles for fun. The other occupants scuffled about in various feral ways. A morning out was good for the soul. And the stomach. Thoughts drifted to dinner. It looked as though they'd make it back for first sittings, when a full menu was still available. Having reloaded the camera, Hewitt tried an arty shot of the iron wheel cast hard against the sky beside the disused pithead. Best half-turned his head towards the rear.

'Well done, all of you. It's been a good morning.'

Even though everyone hated him, they were interested by this attempt at niceness.

'Someone always has to spoil it, though.'

He paused a second while a dread anticipation built up.

'Finimore, you've been smoking. My office at two.'

Finimore never even flinched. No one spoke for the rest of the journey.

At the end of school that day, Hewitt fell in alongside Finimore. Curiosity fuelled, he asked, What did you get?

'Four.'

Bastard.

'Yeah. So What.'

The So What, as Hewitt saw it, was that smoking wasn't such a big deal. Teachers did it. Everyone did it. Finimore was just selected. Somebody was going to get it from Besty and Finimore was that somebody. Besty couldn't bear the idea of a group from the school going out and coming back without a punishment being included in the programme.

Hewitt dragged a stick along the railings on the walk

home, creating a rhythm of dissatisfaction. Unsweet music. In a different mood, you could make a different tune like this.

The next day he and Stevens did their work in the darkroom. The sequence of shots on which Best appeared came out in a neat line of six. Stevens scored the strip delicately, carefully, with a pinhead, establishing an alibi – damaged negatives. They worked over the rest of the film, producing plates deliberately darkened by overdeveloping before fixing the images. The finished work showed stooped old men and women, drenched in shades of grey, receiving food from the youth. At assembly they were commended by Boris the Bold for their exhibition. Hewitt sweated in bed at night, wondering if Best would demand to know why there were no shots of him. He never did.

As the bus drew into the station, Hewitt moved his finger slowly around the interior of the square he'd earlier described on the pane until he could see through it. Another autumn day, but a filthy cold wet one. He imagined Finimore swinging his long limbs across floors, scenting new carpet, securing it around room edges, standing and admiring his work, until he was forty, when his knees would be fucked and he couldn't do it any more.

He bought ten Marlboro from the station stand and, unpeeling the cellophane as he moved to the terminal for the connecting bus down to the Poly, slid his boot through a slick of leaves which the traffic had pushed into the gutter's edge. It's the season of Fall, Stevens, he said.

A Ripple in the Static

As Esme rubs her eyes, flecks of black mascara peel from her lashes and smear along her forefingers. As she attempts to remove the black with her thumbnail, it resists, instead gets into the pores, defining the lines. She scratches the small of her back against the edge of the sink. The kettle comes to the boil, steam condensing on the cream-gloss wall above. Esme pours the water over a teabag in a mug with World's Best Mum printed on it, yawning all the time. And while the brew seeps into the water, Esme takes out the packet from the handbag on the floor, an unfiltered cigarette, taps the end and lights up, reaching over the gas-ring for a flame, straightens, inhales and coughs. She whisks the teabag using a spoon with a crest on the handle, a souvenir from Blackpool, squeezes the bag against the side of the mug, rests the cigarette on the worktop, burning end hanging out, swings round to the bin, steps on the pedal with socked foot and flicks the bag into the liner. A stream of brown liquid, unleashed, splashes up the edge of the unit. Brown drops settle and begin to run down. Caught between first and second finger, ash rising, a lipstick halo defining the previous draw, the cigarette returns to comfort her cracked, wax-coated lips. Esme leans back, opens the fridge door and pulls out the half-empty bottle of sterilized, splashes some into the mug and drops it behind the rail in the door, shuts it with her knee. Two sugars from the bowl on the worktop stirred right in and the spoon goes back, cushioned by the white crystal mound, dripping and deliquescing, setting and softly staining, like a boot dirtying snow.

Esme takes the tea to the back room, eases into the shining brown vinyl armchair and sips. The girls will be back soon. Esme has been awake five minutes. After her morning at the supermarket, she takes an afternoon nap. Wakes up unrefreshed. Joy comes clattering down the back passage. She can tell each of the girls apart by the sound of their footsteps. She kills the fag, spins the butt away into the container below, plunges the handle, the kind you get on a spinning top. The ashtray unsteady on its stand. The last of the smoke hangs, the low sun bleeding through the back window lights it up, a grey and purple falling cloud. The girls don't like her smoking.

Joy comes in quietly. Odd.

'Are you alright, love?' Esme not moving from the chair, Joy in the kitchen.

'Yeah.'

'Come and see us then.'

'Just a minute.'

'What are you up to?'

'Wait. Just a minute.'

A soft rustling from the kitchen. A silence. Esme frowns. Joy tiptoes through, hands behind her back, thick hair in a ponytail, which wasn't how she had it when she left this morning. Freckles dance on her nose, wide, her mouth wears a crook-toothed grin, she steps forward, kisses her mum on the cheek and whips flowers out from behind her back with a flourish.

'Tarr-arr!'

'What are they for, love?' Esme thinking now – it's not Mother's Day or owt like that, is it?

'They're not for anything, they're just for being my mum.'

'You're soft you are. Go get us a vase. Where d'you get them?'

'Never you mind. Here. Vase. I've got water in it already. Come on, where shall we put em? On the sideboard or on the mantelpiece? Sideboard eh?'

And Joy stands back and admires the display. Dead nice. And Joy says, Shift over, mum.

And elbows her mum gently in the side and sits on half the armchair, switches on the stereo, drops the arm to the record, pulls on the headphones and listens as Diana Ross sings, I've got the sweetest hangover, I don't wanna get over.

Then Joy joins in. Esme slides onto the floor. Has our Joy got a lad? she thinks.

Back in the kitchen, Esme makes tea again, times two. Footsteps down the path and she has a third cup going before Amanda even goes by the kitchen window. In she comes fresh and pink, with a perm that made her cry the whole weekend after Auntie Dawn had done it, come round on a Friday with the kit and done it for her, but it is

37

better now. It's not so bad. She's got used to it. It's grow-
ing out a bit.

Amanda drops her bag to the floor, squeezes her mum's
hand and leans back, takes a look at her. Mum looks tired.

'You look tired, mum. I'll do tea.'

'No you won't, and pick that bag up. Put it in your
room.'

Amanda does as she's told then returns.

'I'll do tea, mum. Sit down. Go on. Have a rest.'

'Amanda, I'm alright. I can do tea. *You'll* have homework to do, won't you?'

Their eyes meet at this. Esme's pools of grey chill and
burn like cooling steel. Amanda's, moist, deep dark brown
like her father's, return a second's flash of black fire.

'I'll do it later.'

A still quiet forms between them. Amanda wants to
kiss her mum and make her understand. Joy comes
through, soothing the atmosphere, moaning lightly the
moaning part of the song.

'What's for tea? I'm starving.'

We're cooking. You and me, Amanda replies. Sausage,
egg and chips?

'Yeah! I'll start peeling.'

Esme retreats. Lights a cigarette. She sits down, picks
up the catalogue from off the pouffe. She flicks it through,
clothes, lingerie, shoes, jewellery, pauses at the HiFi, gets
to the furniture. Amanda wants a desk for Christmas.
She closes the book. Squashes the butt flat into the cut-
glass ashtray, a present from Bill's mum, burning her
thumb slightly with the pressure, returns to the kitchen.

'I'll butter some bread.'

I'm buttering the bread, says Joy. You set the table.

Esme does as she's told. The cloth, snapped in the air, sends a ripple through the pink heads of the chrysanthemums standing on the sideboard, before settling to drift, covering the table. She lays cutlery, salt, pepper, sauce – red and brown – and a wicker mat for the teapot. Five cups and saucers.

From the kitchen the music of cooking, hissing as chips hit the fat, and more fat heating in a different key in the frying pan, the pan black and warped with a charred handle. Amanda lowers the sausages, slow and deliberate. They bunch up like logs in a river. She rolls them back and forth with a slice, the skins start splitting.

Esme steps through. Didn't you prick them? she complains.

'I like them bursting, mum. And dad does.'

'I don't know, Amanda.' Esme says the words slowly, shaking her head.

The back door swings open. Sally is home from work. Sally works on the pots. Sally is engaged, to Alex from Sales. Sally speaks to no one, squeezes through the kitchen wrinkling her nose and straight into the bathroom. Emerges five minutes later, her skin glistening with cleanser.

'What's for tea?'

Sausage, Egg and Chips, say Esme, Joy and Amanda in unison. As if she couldn't see anyway.

'Yuck. I'm not eating that.'

Did you have a nice day, love? asks Esme.

'Not specially. Did you get any cottage cheese in?'

'Sorry, love, I forgot. There's some ham.'

'God.' The word spins out, spring-loaded from the back of her throat; she huffs to their room. Their room. Still.

'Now look what you've done.' Esme accuses Amanda.

'Mum, she's always like that. It's Alex.'

Amanda cracks eggs, cracks them with a steel spatula, and finishing the break with one hand, releases the contents of the shells into a Pyrex bowl, feels a bit sick as she watches them slide to the bottom.

The empty sidewalks on
my block are not the same

He's pretending not to see me. He looks alright actually. What's he doing standing on that bench? All the boys are wearing those lumberjack coats right now. It doesn't suit him. But he doesn't look all that bad. He's not too short after all. He's a year above me. An older man.

Hewitt sights her as she turns the corner, but pretends not to. He continues to gaze away towards The Hayes, in a manner he considers highly enigmatic, at the same time clenching his toes, a calming exercise which doesn't work.

Amanda makes her approach up the hill towards the bench on which he stands, with her head tilted slightly down, raising her eyes now and then to confirm, as she nears, that it is him, he has turned up and must have even waited. Oh God. The arrangement to meet has been conducted through Stevens via Amanda's friend Pat via Dionne. The first point of actual contact between them is now. Amanda wears a three-quarter-length coat of dusky blue corduroy. She pulls up three feet from Hewitt, who has stepped down from the bench seven seconds before.

  'Hi.'
  'Hi.'

'Would you like to go to the . . . (Hewitt prevaricates a second, during which time the words cinema/pictures coruscate a million times on his retinas) . . . Cinema?' At each of their homes they call it The Pictures.

'I nearly didn't come. I've been at Pat's. I've been crying, to tell the truth. What's on?'

'That's a really nice coat. I'm glad you did. Come, I mean. I don't know. Let's see when we get there, eh?'

Hewitt knows exactly what's on at all six screens. He's been preparing for three days, since receiving an affirmative on the meeting. He's combined his clothes in four hundred different ways, spent hours in Jean Machine trying to get some trousers that will make his backside look pert.

'Why were you crying?'

'I was frightened, I suppose. I don't know. Why did you ask me out?'

Hewitt couldn't easily answer this. Because you've got beautiful eyes. Because you look shy. Because when I used to watch the netball team practise, it was you I was watching. You played Wing Attack. Because, my sources tell me, and might I say I find this odd, you seem not to have a boyfriend. Because I want you for my girlfriend. Because. Just because.

'Shall we go? To the cinema? I've got money.'

Amanda smiles, for the first time.

Because I love your smile. I've never been this close to it before. You've got a gap between your two front teeth. I love that. It's lucky.

'You've got a gap between your two front teeth.'

I know, she says, *It's lucky.* Is there a bus due? she says.

The Pictures are about three miles away.

'There's one in fifteen minutes. We'll catch it if we go up the walkway. Shall we?'

We, he's thinking, We, Ha. We.

That would be quickest, she says, Wouldn't it? And she looks at him for affirmation.

Yeah. Yes, he replies, smiling, trying, trying not to grin. Keep it cool. Not a stupid smile. He pulls a serious face. He's seen films. He knows the moves.

He wants to hold her hand right now, but he knows it's too soon. What will she be thinking? Will she want him to hold her hand? Link arms maybe. Linking arms is less formal, isn't it, or is it more formal? What is he thinking about, linked arms is for old people. Get a grip.

They walk on orange cinder paths, silicates glint in the moonlight. The ground rises gently ahead. Around the perimeter of the walkway strip, lights twinkle in the windows of the houses. Lights bounce on and off and the space feels theatrical, like something could happen there. Their breath hangs thicker in the air as their bodies warm. Years ago these paths were railway tracks, local ones linking up the pits. Now it's been landscaped, they call it a Model City. It makes the locals laugh.

Hewitt casts his eyes into the sky where a thousand stars pulse and dance.

And Amanda's thinking, He's looking at the stars. Maybe he's romantic.

And Hewitt's thinking the line of a song he's singing to himself. He's singing:

And when the sign beside me points one way,
The light I used to pass by, every day.
Just walk away, Renee, you won't see me follow you back
*   home,*
The empty sidewalks on my block are not the same, you're
*   not to blame.*

It's an old record from home, he plays it sometimes late at night on the radiogram, gazing out the window, smoking, watching the strobing lights from passing traffic. He can't follow the meaning, but he might not have the words right. He doesn't always. He glances right at Amanda. He's on her heart side. From under her soft falling hair an earring shimmers. *He could buy her earrings for a present.*

'When is your birthday?'

Amanda laughs. Her birthday is soon. Amanda leads a conversation about star signs. Hewitt relaxes a bit. This is good. This is going well. Amanda says their two signs are not ideally matched.

'But they're not completely incompatible either. They're somewhere in the middle.'

Hewitt feigns ignorance about all matters star-sign. It's good for Amanda to be able to teach him things. He thinks the best way to attract adoration is to behave a bit clueless here and there.

At the top of the walkway strip they exit through an alley of bushes onto a grey avenue lined with formal semi-detached houses, each one boring in a slightly different way. A short linking road rises off and they take it to emerge onto High Lane. Now they each feel exposed. Anybody could see them here. Hewitt notices for the first time a scent on Amanda. Musk? He could buy her perfume! Unbelievably, this seems like an original thought. Hewitt reaches in his pocket for a cigarette.

'Do you mind if I smoke?'

Amanda doesn't like smoking.

No, suit yourself, she says.

But Hewitt feels self-conscious with the cigarette, because he heard the Yes in the No. He smokes only half before guttering it. To atone he pretends to identify a constellation, the Great Bear. This is an inspired move, because in pointing out the stars which mark the outline he cannot help but offer to touch Amanda, offer to hold her arm out with his, trace her fingers around the shape, a shape he's only just discovering himself.

He's quite nice really. He's going to touch my hand in a minute. He's touching my hand. His hands are cold and slightly damp. Funny. He's brought his face closer. I can smell him. He smells of shampoo and tobacco. He's taking a long time to trace this shape. I can't see it, to be honest. I'm pretending I can though, sort of, a bit. Would I like to kiss him?

They get the top two seats at the front of the bus. A giddy perspective, especially when it stops sharp. Which it does, often. They've got a racing bus-driver. Around them groups of youths display their bravado, smoking and swearing. Lovers snog at the back. A group of girls get on at the stop beside the cemetery, heels clattering against the stairs as they ascend, one hoisting herself up on the coat tail of the one in front like a marionette. Hewitt watches it through the fish-eye mirror above him, the image distorted, the girls small but loud. Over in the cemetery the tombstones list among the trees. Would you rather be buried or cremated? This is not a cool question on a first date. So instead he asks, What does your dad do?

And Amanda tells him with pride that her dad works in a small steelworks, that he makes big parts for . . . she's not sure what, some kind of industry. But that's not the important bit, the important bit is her dad stays on after work and forges things of his own, wrought-iron sculptures. They've got two at home, either side of the fireplace. Amanda loves her dad, Hewitt can tell straight away. Amanda loves all her family. At home, Hewitt is nominally the father figure. His parents are divorced. It's not not normal. Alighting in the centre of town there's a busy road to cross. Pause. Hewitt takes Amanda's hand. Do you mind? he says.

'No.'

She smiles again. The lucky gap.

On the bus home, Hewitt wishes he had a car. It would be more impressive. A silver two-seater sports passes them.

'I'm going to have one of those some day.'

'Do you like fast cars?'

'I like cars.'

'But do you like fast cars?'

Hewitt's never been in a fast car. He pretends he likes fast cars. The open road, man.

'Yeah, sure, fast cars. What do you like?'

'Never thought about it. Our one's a Marina.'

At the top of the hill, three mini-roundabouts connect up, linking about eight roads together. On the edge there, a low garage hoists a neon sign advertising Mercedes-Benz. In the garage tons of gleaming metal shine on pedestals.

I'll buy you a Mercedes-Benz then, says Hewitt, They're good.

And in this lie, Amanda sees their life together. A big house with children, nice things, and a Mercedes-Benz.

At the next stop, two lads get on. Lads Hewitt knew at school. Boys he didn't like, feared a bit even. Insensitive fighting Bastards. As they spot him he has a second to decide either to drop his eyes or catch theirs dead on. He catches theirs dead on. He feels brave. In their eyes, deep and brown, he sees the dead insubordination of future inmates. He can feel them – shall we go for him, embarrass him with his girlfriend? He and Amanda are about a mile from their stop. Hewitt's quick.

'Let's get off here. Can I walk you home? It'll take longer.'

'OK.'

And Hewitt ushers Amanda down the stairs, the lads call him a Wanker, but it's alright, it is alright, he's getting them out in time and Amanda didn't see them look at him when they said it, they could have been abusing anybody upstairs. And now he's got a long walk home with her. A bonus.

He wants to get off the bus early, so we can stay together longer. It was a cool film. He bought the popcorn. He'd look better with his hair cut. I wish I hadn't worn these boots now, they're no good for walking. He's nice. He's quite nice really. Mercedes-Benz.

Hewitt holds her hand again, and though he asks first, she tells him he doesn't have to. He strokes his finger round and round the centre of her palm, the most fascinating and exquisite contour in the world.

Emma lives in a flat in Hackney, over a launderette. She yells Bye whenever she leaves, though there's no one there. Basic burglar protection. Emma has cropped red hair, punkish, and very pale skin. She's a designer. Hewitt works at the same firm as Emma. He's come round tonight to help her move flat, to Kilburn. He's got access to a van. He helps move her rails of clothes, chic market stuff, boxes of records, indie and kitsch. Some furniture, nothing much. A bed. Emma offers Hewitt speed, chops two Lines out on a tile in the bathroom using a credit card. This is a new one for Hewitt. He's been to a couple of parties with Emma, each time she's given him a Line. They snort it up their nostrils using a rolled-up note, washing it down with bottled lager.

OK! Let's go apeshit! says Emma, sniffing caustically, eyes blazing.

After the first time, hours later Hewitt was driving

round the City at five, six in the morning, buzzing, amazed at the wakefulness he still felt, bumping over the cobble-stones in his Mini, lost and laughing.

Hewitt fancies Emma. He likes her unorthodoxy. But he's concerned she's too sophisticated for him. He's worried he might be too, as Emma would say, Mainstream. He's not going to make a move, anyway. He's just going to be around a lot.

It's after midnight, they've finished unloading. Emma sits on a kitchen chair, wraps her legs under her, thanks Hewitt and asks him has he got any dope. Hewitt has some at his place, a mile or so away. He'll go get it.

Good Boy. Emma thinks it and says it too.

After a shared joint, drinking whisky from tall glasses across a papering table, Emma surprises Hewitt.

'Does smoking make you feel horny?'

Even though the dope is killing off the speed a bit, Hewitt's heart beats harder. Fuck.

'Depends who I'm with.'

'What about when you're with me?'

Jesus.

'Well. Could be . . . Yeah. Yes.'

'Good. Where shall we do it then?'

Will the bedroom do for an answer? Or does he need to be more esoteric here?

The garden. The van.

But he doesn't have to say anything because Emma beckons him out of his seat, takes his hand, positions it, kisses him viciously and fucks him right there, standing under the single bare lightbulb in the purple room, with only the essential parts of their clothing peeled back.

Mmm, not bad, she drawls afterwards, There's potential here.

She reaches for a cigarette. Hewitt is elated, though he knows it would not be cool to let this show.

Six months later, Hewitt is walking through Camden Town, trying to avoid going for an early drink. The warm glamour of a second-hand record store draws him in, and while he's flicking through some singles he picks up on the lyric from the music that's playing overhead:

From deep inside the tears I'm forced to hide,
From deep inside the tears I'm forced to cry.
Just walk away, Renee, you won't see me follow you back
*   home.*
The empty sidewalks on my block are not the same.
You're not to blame.

He thinks he's worked it out. It's a song about forgiveness. He thinks about Amanda for the first time in a long time. Pausing at the threshold, Hewitt surveys the scene. Out on the street an array of freaks walk by. Traffic thunders noiselessly past. Up in the sky, not a single star pulses or dances. He could go back. Maybe this would be the right time for it.

Bubble Gum

The girl behind the counter blows bubbles with her gum. An irregular sphere emerges, inflates and punctures in rhythm with her chewing. The man in front makes his purchase. One ready meal, a packet of frozen mince, a white sliced loaf, two cans of lager. She checks them through, glances up.

'And your Rothmans?'

'Please, love.'

The girl is the owner's eldest daughter. The three other children make a playground of the shop, roller-skating up and down. The serving girl's skin is pale brown, hair black, held back in a band. She wears a nylon apron. In her make-up and turquoise nail varnish, under the faint purple neon, her beauty beguiles. I focus. My turn.

Have you got any lemons? I ask. I couldn't find any.

A bubble collapses over her lips, encasing them for a second. She scrolls the gum back in, twisting it round her tongue.

'Got Jif.'

That'll do. I half turn. Where?

She calls to one of the roller-skaters.

'Kev, bring a squeezy lemon down, will ya?'

Kev ducks, rises, ducks again, comes hard out of the

corner, applies the brake, feet sideways on, pulling up the coolest half-inch from my toe.

'Ereyago.'

His grin a mix of couldn't care and dare, he deposits a yellow plastic lemon into my palm.

Ta. I turn back to the girl. How much?

'Eighteen.'

Handing over the right money, I pick up a packet of gum, so I can prolong my study of her.

How much is this?

'Ten.'

I give her fifty. She keeps her eye on a drunk at the far end while she uses the till. Kev has gone back up there to patrol, but Kev's swirling presence is only irritating the man, like a gnat in his peripheral vision. He lashes out. An aimless sweep of his arm misses Kev by miles. Kev laughs. The girl shouts at him to stop annoying the man. He gives her the Vs and glides into the back through the tasselled curtain. The girl sucks air in through her teeth and shakes her head.

Always up to something he is, she says, Here, your change. She doesn't look up.

Outside, I toss the juice into the air, the spinning yellow falling in slow-mo. Repeating the toss, this time trying a reverse catch behind my back, I miss. As I lean into the gutter to retrieve it, my whites get splashed by a passing truck.

Cheers Mate.

Back in Tim's Fiat Junkheap Special I'm tempted to motor off into the hills. But I need my wages. I drive the half-mile back to the restaurant.

◆

Round the back I skid to a stop on the gravel, just short of
the herb bed. Tim leans against the wall, reading the
Guardian, doesn't bat an eye. In through the door, I lay my
cigarette on the window-sill, the burning end resting out.
When I return later, it's smouldered away; I flick the filter
through the horizontal column of ash, the particles mote,
the filter somersaults across the concrete, a near full-
length nicotine burn taking its place on the ledge in a cigarette pantheon. Chefs never smoke a full fag, not whilst
on duty anyway. Apart from Nick, who as Head Chef is
allowed to smoke and work simultaneously. Nick turns
from the oven.

'You took your time. D'ya get that fucking[1] lemon?'

Got Jif.

'Fuckin' hell.'

T's all I could get. It is Easter Monday, y'know.

'Chuck the fucker over then.'

I chuck the fucker over. Nick squirts juice onto smoked
salmon shining on its bed of curly lettuce, hemmed
around by quartered tomatoes and radish petals. A dish
distinguished by an absence of quartered lemons. He
showers more over a prawn cocktail.

'Table two away.'

On the other side of the hotplate, Roberto stubs his fag
(the waiters smoke on their side, it's up to them if they get
caught, we don't care), picks up the two plates, stacks
them on his arm in a two-tier arrangement.

1 The swearing might seem gratuitous in this story. It is included in the interests
of accuracy. All chefs swear all the time.

'Prawn cocktail, smoked salmon. Fucking[2] peasants.'

On top of the fridge, an old Roberts broadcasts Piccadilly Radio from Manchester. Dr Hook's If I Said You Had a Beautiful Body Would You Hold It Against Me floats in the steam. The bain-marie, the hobs, the oven and the water foaming in the deep steel sink where Alfie does the washing-up contribute gently or furiously to steam production. Life's a sauna. Alfie was recruited from the asylum up the road. At first he returned there at night, but he's charming, so the owners have taken him on as a member of the family. He lives in, upstairs in a tiny attic room. He's covered the walls completely with Manchester United pictures, posters, pennants and stickers. Though they no longer play, Best and Charlton are the stars of Alfie's gallery. Alfie told us one day that his dad was buried in Strangeways, a prison for serious offenders. Nick was amazed, he told me that the only way you got buried in prison was if you were a lifer, which meant Alfie's dad must have murdered somebody. Fuck.

Fucking right, said Nick.

Alfie's head rocks from side to side when he gets excited, when the dirty crockery piles in at the busiest times – Saturday nights and Sunday lunches and weddings. The busier it is, the more his head rocks. Nick says we should attach Brillo pads to his ears and stick him in the oven to clean it out. I'm a student of casual cruelty. Would we have the oven turned on or off?

Bugger off and gut that box of trout over there, says Nick.

2 Waiters too.

54

Trout gutting is the second-worst appalling job. Removing the innards of pheasants is the first-worst. Trout guts are cold and slimy and hard to get a grip of. Pheasant guts, after the birds have been hanging for a couple of weeks, stink like hell, and are lumpy and gristly and slimy. I also have to hack the necks off. Here we find undigested corn, and stuff which is even worse. I'm a Commis Chef, part time. A Commis is like an apprentice. Commis is Kitchen French. Being a Commis means I am entrusted with all the Special Shit Jobs. Or *travail merde* as Tim the Great Intellectual calls them. *Beaucoup de travail merde pour vous, petit fuckère*, he says, banging a hundredweight of sprouts sacked up in a green nylon stocking onto the worktop for me to peel. And as well as peeling them, I have to score a little cross into the underside of each one in order that the tougher bit at the bottom absorbs the boiling water so the sprouts cook through evenly. Nick carries out random checks and gives me a flicky if he finds one uncrossed. A flicky's a flicked ear. It's sore: chefs have tough hands, they're not poofs. Nick won a cucumber-slicing competition last year. It was held at the Railway Hotel. You have to slice as many cucumbers as possible in one minute. The winner decided by how many cucumbers get sliced multiplied by how many slices to the inch. You need strong wrists. Me and Tim went along, we were cheering Nick on like Stoke were playing in the FA Cup Final (or Man City in Tim's case).

When I say chefs aren't poofs that's not quite right about Nick, because he is. It's Nick's son Jasper, or Jasper the

Rasper as he prefers to be known, who mostly draws attention to this. Jasper helps out on particularly busy weekends, doing tasks even more menial than the ones I do. When Nick irritates him, he's been known to tell him to Fuck Off[3] You Poof or call him a Fuckin' Queer Git.

Nick takes this well, instructing him to Stop Moaning You Little Bastard – technically incorrect as Nick is still married to Jasper's mum and still lives with her and Jasper's brothers. I never call him a Poof or a Queer Git. Just Nick.

The smoked salmon follows up with *caneton à l'orange*, but the prawn-cocktail companion takes us by surprise with an *escalope de veau viennoise* – thin slices of veal garnished with chopped egg-white, chopped egg-yolk, chopped parsley, an anchovy fillet and a stoned olive. And a slice of peeled lemon. Nick is impressed by this somewhat *outré* selection, so applies the Jif sparingly and precisely. That's about it for tonight, it's been dead slow. I've been doing some *mise-en-place* for the week ahead, making crème caramels and sponge cakes. Tim left, bored, to do something arty in the Fiat JS a while back.

As Roberto knocks off, he gives banter about seeing if he can get any life out of the missus, as he'll be home early.

You'll more likely disturb her with her lover, Nick says. Probably some dyke looking at the state of you, Roberto.

Roberto smiles and tells him, in waiter Spanish, to go fuck his mother. We clean up, get changed upstairs, take a

3 Chefs' sons also.

whisky each from the bar, large ones, lock up. Nick runs me home. We drive round a peninsula of scrub, from the other side of which we can see the restaurant lit up on the skyline. The neon sign reads The Cross Keys. Nick puts on his Rod Stewart tape, A Night on the Town. Rod's a prat, but I can't help liking the songs. Nick yawns, stretches.

I think I'll go to the club, he says.

He's come out with this a few times before but I've never followed it up. He doesn't name the club, though I know where he means. To continue to grunt at this remark/overture is becoming difficult. I suck my breath through my teeth. What club?

'The One-2-One.' Pause. 'Do you want to come?'

Why not? Let's see what it's like. Alright.

And Nick smiles at me sidelong. He's got tight-cut hair, grey and brown; he wears John Lennon glasses. He's wiry and trim, professional-looking. I keep my gaze fast through the windscreen, pull out a cigarette. My heart beats. We're silent for a couple of miles, just listening to the music, The Killing of Georgie, with that spine-tingle break in the middle followed by the requiem.

A requiem in a fucking pop song, brilliant, Nick said the first time he played it when we were in the kitchen.

Tim said he was testing me to see if I knew what requiem meant. We roll down a long, straight, shallow hill, intersected at right angles a little over half-way down by an equally straight road which passes under it. The lights below cast away to vanishing point in each direction. A turn at the bottom leads us in through the low sprawl of the city centre. Low, that is, aside from a few tower blocks. Someone from my school knew someone who died falling from a balcony from one of those blocks. Some guys he was chasing after for some reason pushed him over. He wasn't old enough to have died. I didn't actually feel that much about it. I didn't know him very well, but I remember going to a school swimming gala with him once, walking along with our bags and everything across the park, buying fish and chips afterwards on the way home. He was a bit older than us. He was alright. I felt like I should have felt something more about him dying.

The One-2-One looks like a warehouse. It hasn't got a sign, or anything else that would let you know it was a club. I've never been here before, and actually I didn't even know this was where it was. It's opposite a supermarket. We park down a side-street. I walk well away from Nick, I don't want him taking me by the arm or anything. Round the side of the building, Nick notices a fire-escape door ajar and, muttering fucks, closes it with his toe. We enter through a corrugated door – you can scarcely pick it out from the remainder of the corrugated surface – and pass down a corridor, negotiating several doors on the way, each of which is opened for us and closed behind by Security, all of whom know Nick, give him a friendly greeting, look me over and shift to innuendo. Oh fuck.

We arrive at a paying-in desk. Nick is virtually on the staff by now, and first things first informs them of the danger implied by the open fire escape. A bit of alarm is generated by this news, and someone goes to check that it's properly shut now. I'm realizing Nick's a celeb. We don't even have to pay entrance. Inside, I'm stunned. I mentioned Nick's appearance. He's wearing regular clothes too, in the way of a wiry and trim professional-looking chef. As we press through, we part a tide of men who must be off-duty builders in drag. One guy holding court in the middle of the bar has on a clingy, sequinned, turquoise top slit to the navel, white high-waisters (high-waisters are out of fashion and have been for years, but White ones . . .) and cerise platform boots. He's got big, big bouffant hair, and make-up. You can't walk around like that round here; how the fuck did he get in alive? Nick buys drinks. Free drinks might be the reason I'm here, I'm beginning to think, and if I was older I might feel a bit shabby about it. We move over to some of Nick's friends in the corner.

'Who is This pretty little boy, Nick?'

'I don't think we've seen You before.'

Nick introduces, and I don't know exactly what to do or how to behave. I respond in instinctive schoolboy manner by sliding round the group and getting my back to the wall. Fuck, fuck, fuck. This must be what it's like being a girl. Nick is issuing calming instructions, telling them to let me settle down a bit, you know, it's his first time here and all that. It gets worse. I start seeing faces I recognize. There's a bloke over the other side who used to work on a stall in the market where I worked when I was younger. He's got make-up on too. Unbelievable. And now, I'm realizing, if he sees me he'll think, Ah-ha, what's all this then? I do the brave, sensible thing and sidle out of view.

Time passes too slowly. I manage to laugh when the boys

get all bitchy about the girls, Fucking Dykes. (It's actually mixed sexes, this club). But really all I want to do is get out. I feel hunted and I don't want to be. Nick encourages, shepherds, shields, cajoles. It's perfectly normal, you know. But eventually he gives in to my discomfort and takes me home.

On the drive back, we discuss who was who back there. My polite interest is a façade. Outside my house, he switches off the ignition, puts his hand on my knee. My own hands recoil into my jacket pockets. I find the bubble-gum, pull it out, unwrap a piece, start chewing. This must be fantastically unsexy, this chewing, I think, I hope, while saying, No, it's never occurred to me actually, really, honest, no, not even mutual masturbation. No. I unpeel myself from the car, and as Nick's tail-lights fade, blow a bubble, which pops as it punctures.

Hello Sunshine

Grandad Bill: The Preliminary Notes

1 He was the first person anywhere in the world to own a Ford Zephyr. Maroon and grey. The bench seat.

2 He once took me to the races and put me a shilling on Double Diamond, which came in at twenty to one. I won one whole pound note. More money than you can ever dream of.

3 He was the first person round our way to get a hair-piece. De luxe.

4 He always carried a great fat wad of notes.

5 He had an impossibly glamorous girlfriend. She was younger. Everybody said she was only after him for his money. I got to sit by her on the bench seat.

6 On Tuesdays he brought fish and chips over and we ate them in front of the telly, with Dick Dastardly and Muttley. Rashnsashnfashn.

7 Once, on a Good Friday, I helped on his fruit and veg stall. It was an outdoor market. At about ten in the morning it started snowing. By lunchtime the snow

was thick on the ground and thick on the stall. Every time somebody asked for mushrooms he whispered, More snow in with them mushrooms, Sunshine. Every pound of mushrooms was half a pound of snow. He thought it was dead funny. Me too.

8   He knew Jimmy Greenhoff. Jimmy Greenhoff was our centre-forward. I got his autograph. And to speak to him. And to see the dressing rooms.

9   He took me to an away Cup-tie at Huddersfield.

10 And to another at Old Trafford.

11 Grandad Bill swapped the Zephyr for a Jag. I can't remember what colour that was. You don't get many Jags round our way.

12 He was out of my league now.

Sweet

I can't revise any more. I know nothing any more. I want to know no more of salmonella, botulism or any other food-poisoning agent. I can remember no formula which will be a starch. Starches are polysaccharides, sugars that is. I *can* remember that. I do know about raffinose, the sugar which breaks down turbulently, creating flatulence. That's an easy one to remember.

I'm going to go out, to the Town Hall. The Jam are playing tonight. I didn't get a ticket in advance because of it being exam week. But this afternoon, when I finally cracked and went to the record shop, they had two returns. *Two*. I could only afford one. I've been fingering it ever since, checking it's still there in my pocket. It already looks like it's been through the wash.

Concert-Going Outfit: old school blazer, old school tie. Lodger's shirt, white with pleated front. Dogtooth trousers. Winklepickers (mail order through the NME. Too tight). Marlboro (10). Penknife.

Standing at the stop queuing and jigging. When it comes, the bus is wild. Today, Tuesday lunchtime, The Jam went straight in at number one with a song called Going Underground. The Radio One DJs never played it, but there it is, straight in at number one and on the bus we can feel power. Power. We put it there and those jerks with their shaggy haircuts and comedy specs don't have a clue. And now they'll have to play it, This Week's Number One, and we'll be laughing, knowing they hate it and they had nothing to do with it, it's not their hot tip of the week. Not their tune, our tune.

I get off two stops early to pick up a quarter-bottle of Smirnoff. Craig Mitchell gets off with me. Mitchell's a punk. I'm a punk/mod. It's alright. Mitchell buys cider and Mars Bars. We stroll across three wide lanes of banking tarmac, a racing-track piece of road, ignoring the horns, not even bothering to give the finger. In the car park of Lewis's department store we stop to admire a Vespa. Lewis's has a massive, spiky, alien steel figure, must be thirty feet tall, bolted to the front, high above the main doors – a creature somewhere between the Statue of Liberty and Kiss. I'm just waiting for the Evening Sentinel Disaster Special Edition on how the emergency services coped when it broke free and plunged, impaling 39 shoppers, 53 carrier bags, a double-decker bus and a drayman's horse. We drop round the back of the Gaiety for a laugh, where heavy rockers spill onto the back yard, admiring each other's bikes, drinking piss and tamely mocking our appearance. State of them.

Greeboes.

You fucking relics, shouts Mitchell.

So we have to run. Mitchell's an idiot. I don't like him.

Outside the hall, we're way back in the queue. Queuing

starts at lunchtime for these gigs, to ensure priority position right at the front, in the serious mêlée area. Or just for something to do, to kill time. About a hundred people ahead I can see our kid. Green hair this week. Our kid makes Mitchell seem as smart as a Mensa candidate. Gets into more trouble in a day than anybody else could in a week. There's always a girl with him, though. He's a got a Siouxsie Sioux tonight, and he's wearing the punkest outfit you'll see round here. I back up against the wall so he won't see me. If he does, he'll only shout across that I'm a Tosser or something, then I'll have to beat him up later. I can't be bothered. I'm getting too old for beating up my younger brother. It's too embarrassing. And anyway The Security could get involved, and other people would join in, and I might get beaten up myself – I'd miss the gig, etc. I unscrew the cap and pull on the vodka, wincing. Suddenly I've got friends. I pass it on and it never comes back. Leaning forward again, I see our kid standing on the railings, singing, using his tie for a mic. Freckle-faced fool.

When I was little, I was having my hair cut at the barber's at the bottom of Pittshill bank, just up from the cobbler's. It was the haircut my dad really hated, a crewcut. The barber's was like somebody's front room and the barber was an old grey-haired man, the back of his neck red raw, looking like he gave it a daily shave with the ttzzz trimming machine. He wore a brown overall and smelt of Vitalis. I was slightly more frightened by him than I was by the dentist. But not as much as by visits to the clinic, where one-eyed children wearing pink perforated eyepatches would come out from round corners. The eye you could see was called a Lazy Eye, for which this patch-wearing was the cure. It meant the eye you could see might be looking anywhere.

He wants a crewcut, my mum said. This sounded exotic, made me think it was something to do with sailors. It was a long skinhead. I hear your Paul's been in trouble again, the barber says to mum. Paul and his mate Phil had spent a Sunday morning pulling up somebody's picket fence. Not Huckleberry Finn whitewash, not that sort of fence; it was a series of creosote-coated stakes banged into the ground, each stake linked to its neighbour by a piece of twisted wire. The fence went right round some old misery's allotment, it was a long one. The boys uprooted most of it before they got caught. My dad spent all that afternoon, and nights the rest of the week, repairing the damage. Construction work takes longer than destruction work. He's a bit of a handful, mum replies, with mixed pride and wonder. I can just about remember this because I was about six, which means Paul was four. I wonder where he was right then? He might have been out establishing a career as a budding business failure. When I was five and had just started school, so he was three and a half and hadn't, he took my go-kart out into the street and swapped it with two Banksiders, big boys, he said (who must have been skiving off), for a shilling. That's five new pence. He bought gobstoppers from Mrs Reardon's with the money. The go-kart was new, not a home-made, it was yellow, it had pedals and a steering wheel and black and white chequered stripes on the frame. It must have been worth at least a tenner even then. I wasn't too chuffed when I got home. I never knew starting school would have side effects.

I peer round down the line. He hasn't dropped his trousers yet, anyway. He's lying down, all nonchalant, like he's a bit tired and has seen it all before. Siouxsie Sioux is sitting on top of him exploring his cavities with her tongue. There'll be plenty of them, he never goes to the dentist and he lives on sugar butties.

Inside it's all peeled paint and fading glory, powdering plasterwork. Dull gilt. Proms or something should happen here. Council meetings. The only thing I know for sure that happens regularly is the wrestling on a Saturday night. I went with Frank a couple of times. From behind trestle tables in the corridors, rock-tour glamos sell T-shirts. That looks like it could be a good job. The corridors run round the perimeter of the main hall, which is big, lit by chandeliers, smoky. The seating in the stalls is removed for these concerts. People sit and squat on the boarded floor, drinking beer from uncooled cans. A gallery runs around the top, supported by columns which don't look quite substantial enough for the job. The gallery shakes when the dancing starts. It's another thing I always expect to fall down. At the front, the stage back-drop is a quartered black and white banner, billowing gently behind the drum riser. Banks of speakers form black columns at each front edge. The smell is leather. Mitchell's still with me, and we take our turn abusing appearances. There are some old people around who will come to any concert, whoever it is. They wear denim jackets with band name-badges sewn on, Genesis, Yes and all that rubbish. The women wear tight leggings or jeans tucked into snakeskin boots. The blokes have ponytails. Some of them have moustaches. Appalling. The lights drop and the backing band turn up. They've got a slinking lead singer who thinks she's sexy. She isn't. They're about as bad as any normal backing band. Hardcore types still pogo down at the front anyway. Wolfwhistles and abuse.

Fuck off, you're rubbish, shouts Mitchell after about three songs.

The ponytails and the snakeskins look at him disapprovingly. I can see our kid and Siouxsie pressed against the balcony rail near the stage edge. He's punching the air, shouting things, trying to upstage the band. His dim mate with the ginger Mohican is with him, wearing his mum's jumper for a shirt. Before the backing band go, the slinking singer calls out, The Jam are my favourite band, are they yours? This question rightly receives a hail of beer cans. I watch our kid gob at her from his perch. He always was a good spitter. The backing band go. Thank God.

INTERVAL

The house lights go down once more. Mania. Every song an exorcism. One hour of fire on fire. An hour's all you get with this kind of band. How do Two guitars and One set of drums make so much NOISE. Mitchell's jumping up and down off my back, using me as a vaulting horse. I elbow the moron in the cods to get him off and squeeze forward. To squeeze forward you have to get down low, between the legs – people don't want you in front of them; you should've got there early like they did and staked out your ground hours ago. I manage to get close into the fringe of the vortex at the stage front, bodies whirling and leaping and splatting off each other. Sweat and spit flying. I join in, sort of, just at the edge. I keep getting bounced and rolled and rolled and bounced, and I'm moving to the side, round to the speaker stack, as if I was in a rapid. I lean into some bodies, trying to get a look at the band's footwear, so I know what I need to be buying. Overhead something's happening, attracting my attention away from the stage. Our kid's being dangled from the balcony by the ginger Mohican, who's holding him by the arms, like they're trapeze artists. He's swinging pendulum style, his legs kicking back and forth, as far as his new bondage trousers will allow.

Jump, Jump, Jump. Jump you Fucker Jump, I hear someone shout.

Cat, I'm saying to myself. It's my new word for Oh Fuck. Paul Robbins made it up. Cat Cat Cat. I squirm back into the numbers, not wanting to see. The crowd might catch him. Then again they might not. I surface beside Mitchell, turn to look back, our kid's disappeared.

What happened? I shout.

They pulled him back up. Mitchell's spittle flies into my cheek, He's a stupid twat, in't he?

He is.

I forget about our kid and I let go, give in to the volume, pogo. Outside, after, I've sweated so much that when I pull my blazer off the arm tears right away. It must've rotted or something. I walk the three miles home in my white dinner shirt and my school tie, with my one arm missing, dreaming dreams of being on stage. I pass by three or four pubs, low two-storey buildings designed like ocean liners, cruising on the edges of estates. Sometimes, when I can't find anything else to do, I go into one or two of these and watch the bands play on a weekend night. Club Bands. I did it My Way. Someone my mum knows plays the drums. If you're really pissed it's alright.

I let myself in. At the breakfast bar, with a bowl of cornflakes, I read Smash Hits. Our kid arrives twenty minutes later and organizes the same food, pours two tons of sugar on his, straight from the bag. He's full of it.

'Did you see me?'

I pretend I never noticed.

The exams are not a total fuck-up.

INTERVAL

We didn't see much of each other and we hardly kept in touch. We lived in different cities. We did various jobs. One day I got a call on the telephone, early in the morning.

What's up? I said straight off.

Something would have to be up for my mum to call at this time of day. She told me our kid was in hospital in intensive care, he'd taken a big fall off a building, doing something he shouldn't have been doing. I wasn't surprised. I was pissed off with him. Mum was in a state. I got to see him in hospital a few weeks later. I didn't want to go there and give him a hard time when he was still really ill – well, when I got there he had too much ironmongery in him for me to give him the hard time. He was rigged up with precision scaffolding, threaded rods were screwed into him, his limbs were fixed into position by universal joints. He was keen to show me how all this kit worked, I was interested. He pulled the sheet back. He knew I was pissed off with him. I didn't have to say it.

ENCORE

I went down to help him out with a job. Building work. He was into that kind of thing and needed a hand. It was sweltering summer. We each had our shirts off, his body had scars from the accident all over, his skin looked like an abstract canvas. He spent days stripping paint from old window frames, burning off the gluey layers, getting back the wood. It smelt good. I coloured the walls. He told stories, about himself mostly, about things I didn't know about. They were funny stories, and sometimes sad too.

At night when we went for a beer, he walked with a limp. I had to walk a little behind him on the pavement so he didn't keep rolling his shoulder into mine. One of the nights he took a scooter out of his van, the kind of scooter kids play on, with a low platform that you stand on with one foot, pushing yourself along with the other. This one had a little motor attached, it could do maybe twenty, twenty-five miles an hour. There was an accelerator lever on one handle and a brake on the other. They were a new thing here, he told me, from America. He cruised up and down the street outside the pub, weaving between the traffic and the people. He pulled up.

'Go on, have a go.'

I loved it, ridiculous machine with its wailing motor. I loved its basic-ness. I loved the warm wind on my face, shifting the dust. It's brilliant, I said when I stopped, leaning it against the table outside, making the pints spill a bit.

Sweet, he said.

I looked at him. We lifted our drinks and clinked glasses.

'I've been pulled by the police a few times on it, but they can't work out what to charge me with.'

I had another go. He was watching me and smiling. He thinks I'm too uptight most of the time. I coasted to a stop once more and sat down.

'Sweet Big Bro.' Still smiling. 'Sweet as a nut.'

That's what he says now when I give him a call. But he always did. How's it going, our kid?

Sweet. Sweet as.

Stitches

Breaks and lunchtimes there are two gangs – Booth's gang and Littleton's gang. Booth is harder. His gang is the best to be in. But Littleton has charisma, he has a louche, baby-faced charm and a shock of yellow hair. He is short and wideish. Booth is skinnier, with tight ginger hair. He's a good runner. He gets the good runners into his gang. His gang are fast. There is chasing and fighting. More often than not Littleton's gang lose, but it's more fun to be in. Littleton's leadership style tends to the laissez-faire. The suspicion exists that if you are in Booth's gang you might be expected to put in extra training after school – drilling, or learning combat skills or something.

Outside school, the gangs can amalgamate when threatened by a mutual enemy, i.e. Banksiders and/or Heath-Enders. Wars are organized on the walkways. One early summer night, during one of these skirmishes, Littleton loses pieces of his two front teeth to a catapulted golf ball. His upper lip and gum explode, he's spitting fragments of tooth and blood. He ducks down and lays back against a bank of grass, feeling in his mouth with his forefinger. Does it need stitches? It might, you know, it might. It looks bad. Better get off up the Hayward, to casualty. No. You'd better. You better had.

The Hayward smells of antiseptic and cough sweets. Reminds you of when you had to have your injections at the clinic. Littleton sits on a bench, holding his mouth, dirt and mud and blood staining his shirt sleeve. There's a poster sellotaped to the wall showing pictures of teeth, roots and all, with advice about the best way to brush them, the best brushes and toothpastes to use. Suddenly a nurse. Why do they always wear their watch there, around their strap? 'What have you been up to?' Nowt. 'Funny sort of nowt that winds up with a mess like this, isn't it?' Littleton says nothing. Safest. 'Come on, let's get a look at you then.' Littleton is hoisted up and set onto a green leather couch, while the nurse cleans his face with warm, damp cotton wool. I hope mum doesn't find out. I'll be in for it then alright. A doctor arrives. 'Shall we put a stitch in it, doctor?' the nurse says. The doctor leans down and peels back Littleton's lip with his thumb. Littleton tries not to wince too much. Don't show it, don't show it's hurting. 'Hmm. Probably heal just as well without. Been fighting, have you?' Littleton looks at the floor. The doctor, he's a good bloke though, because he just tousles the boy's hair. 'Haven't we seen you in here before?' Don't know. Littleton stares at the doctor's stomach, the bobbled surface of his tie zooming backwards and forwards making his eyes go funny. 'Well, try not to let us see you in here again, eh?' Littleton grunts. The nurse says, 'D'you hear what the doctor said?' Yeah, yeah. Littleton rolls his eyes up at the nurse. Come on, let me out.

Three of the gang are waiting. Y'alright? What happened? Did you get stitches?

I'm alright. It's nothing. Nah, it didn't need it.

They leave the hospital grounds through the rhododendron bushes, weaving in and out, stalking something that's not there. On the main road they keep their wits sharp, looking out over the football pitches down the way for any Banksiders who might still be about. They see one another home, taking a route through alleyways littered with cardboard boxes of rubbish, which they jump on and splatter. They catburgle over the rooftops of the garages till Littleton is the last one left. He doesn't fancy home, not yet, so he snakes up Francis Street, turns into Roseberry Street at the top and stops beside the third terrace after the passage. Auntie Vick's. Auntie Vick is married to Littleton's eldest brother Philip. Philip is twenty-one and Craig, his other brother, is eighteen. Littleton has been standing on the pavement with his mum many a time when she's been talking with somebody and let on that, with him, she got caught with a late one. Littleton doesn't like Phil, but it's alright because he knows Phil will have left for the nightshift by now. He likes Auntie Vick. He'll probably be able to go in for a bit. He climbs three steep stone steps, stretches for the bell, it's right at the top, black with a red button. It's new. Tring . . . tring . . . tring . . . tring . . . Auntie Vick pulls the door back sharp, she looks cross and all untidy. Tut tut tut, she clicks her tongue, 'What are you doing here?' Littleton tries to speak without opening his mouth, he doesn't want her noticing his missing teeth. Just y'know, he says, looking

sideways and down. 'I suppose you want to come in?'
Course. 'Get along then.' He squeezes through the hall,
looking for the kitchen. 'Hungry are we?' Auntie Vick
looks down over Littleton and he swings round. Yeah.
'Whatever have you done to your teeth?' Bugger – forgot
to keep me mouth shut. Oh, er, nothing. 'Nothing! Good
God. Does your mum know? She doesn't, does she?
Heaven alone knows what she'll say when she sees the
state of ya. Christ. Does it hurt?' Auntie Vick kneels
down and has a good look. The cut inside the lip has
developed into a succulent mauve weal. The right front
tooth meets the left front tooth half-way to the gum, making a jagged-edged A. 'Eeeh,' she sighs, 'it looks even
worse at close quarters.' She straightens. 'Be a pig's foot
in the morning.' Will it? Shit. 'What are we going to give
you then? Rice pudding?' Please. Can I have jam in it?
She opens the tin, tips the pudding into the little
saucepan, puts the saucepan on the front ring, lights the
gas, pulls the red jam down from the cupboard. 'Did you
go up the hospital?' Yeah. 'What did they say?' Said it'd
be alright without a stitch. Auntie Vick pours the rice
pudding into a bowl, a bowl with blue and white horse-
drawn coaches driving round its edge. The part of the
spoon you eat from is fan-shaped, like the kind of wafer
you get from the ice-cream man. Littleton likes these
spoons. He sits in the chair by the window, Auntie Vick
picks up some knitting from the dining-room table and
settles in opposite. She's making a tiny white jacket. She's
having a baby. She asks Littleton a lot of questions about
what he's been up to, but he doesn't do much answering,
he just watches the tips of the knitting needles flashing

under Auntie Vick's control. Click-clack, click-clack, click-clack. He cleans the edge of the bowl with the wafer spoon, licking the last of the jam with his fingers. 'Damn.' What's up, Auntie Vick? 'Dropped a stitch.' What's that mean? 'It means a bit of the wool fell off the end of the needle.' Can you mend it? 'Yes. It's a nuisance though. Have you finished that pudding?' Yeah. 'Had enough?' Yeah. 'Is it still hurting?' A bit. Not much. 'Better get off home, hadn't you?' Suppose.

Before he leaves, Auntie Vick pulls him under the kitchen strip-light and swabs his mouth out with a wet flannel. He squirms. 'Hold still,' she says. She wipes the rest of his face gently. 'Hmm,' she says, 'If you go in round the back and straight up the stairs your mum mightn't notice.'

Littleton troops up the bank. There's a roundabout at the top, a chip van parks beside it at night. He can see the roof of it from here, steam coming out of the funnel. Sometimes he's got enough on him for chips, peas and gravy. They come in a tray with a wooden fork. On the corner is a corner shop which sells ciggies, cornflakes, bleach, sandwiches and pies. A big fat man who smells owns it. Across, opposite, there's a pub, the window panes are tinted and give out an orange light. Littleton crosses the road, he wants to pull himself up by the pub window-sill to see if his cousin Jeff's in. If he is, Jeff will get him Vimto and crisps. Half-way across there's a concrete bed with a pair of white plastic columns with yellow lights at the top. A traffic island. The columns are about boy-height. Littleton walks between the two of them, and as he steps out onto the second half of the road a motorist hits his brake pedal like he's never done before, and the car seems almost to stop in time. The bumper nudges the child hard and catapults him dead vertical, he loops-the-loop, falls back to the bonnet and bounces into the road, landing on his backside. By the time the driver is out Littleton is standing, brushing himself down. 'What do you think you're doing hiding behind those islands like that?' the driver demands. Sorry, mister. 'What are your parents doing letting you out at this time of night, eh?' It's not their fault. I'm late. I should be home by now. Don't tell 'em. Please. 'Well . . . maybe not this time. But don't let me catch you doing that again. Right?' Yeah, yeah. 'Are you OK anyway?' Yeah. I'm good at landing.

'Well then . . .' The driver pauses, hands on hips, gets back into his car, starts the engine. He waves to Littleton as he pulls away and Littleton waves back. Littleton feels in his pocket. His money's still there. He's just got enough for chips and gravy. After he's bought them, he walks away down the other side, eating.

He finishes them off just around the corner from home and gets rid of the wrapper in Mrs Alcock's hedge. Outside his house he can see the light from the TV switching back and forth, a grey and lilac flicker dancing through the nets. Good. If they're watching telly he's got a chance. He sneaks in through the back door, pulls it to softly, really gently, tiptoes to bed. He gets undressed, slips his pyjamas from under the pillow, puts them on without washing and slides between the sheets. On one wall of his room is a big Disney mural Craig did – a scene with all the characters from Jungle Book. Mowgli's hanging from a branch by one arm. Littleton knows some trees where you can do that, over the back they are, towards Knyp Pool. He thinks about skiving off tomorrow, going to play by the water and the trees. Then he remembers his teeth and all that. The dressing table in the corner supports a swing mirror. He gets close up to it and pulls back his lip like the doctor and Auntie Vick did. Impressive. Something to show. Booth won't try it on when he sees that. I'll go in after all.

Two years later, Littleton is dead. He doesn't die from his lifestyle activities. He gets cancer. He still goes to school most of the time. When all his hair falls out he wears a bobble hat. And nobody takes the piss. In assembly, when they announce it, everybody, even Booth, cries.

Stepping Stones

Summer holidays we'd cycle into the Peaks. Four or five of us on eight or ten wheels – mean machines, some of us with a low centre of gravity, a long bench seat in lean-back black vinyl, a flagpole tethered to the chrome backrest hoisting a fabric triangle (Easy Rider). Others of us were forced into a stiff-backed posture, curiously off-balance, gripping cow horns in the semi-crucifixion position, plastic streamers flaring; lollipop sticks wedged in the forks played tunes on the spokes.

Super-accessorized with carriers, badges, horns, stickers, water-bottles, handlebar tape, fingerless racing gloves et al, we cavalcaded out of the city, jumping lights and raiding bakers' shops. The first long haul uphill, as urban switched through suburban, switched past motor showrooms and petrol stations, switched past the remand centre, switched beside the slaughterhouses at Cellarhead and into Real Country, switched into first arguments.

'Wait for me.'

'Don't go so fucking fast.'

'S'right. You'll only be knackered later, I'm telling you.'

At the beginning, the led will catch up with Leader because Leader will tire but he won't let this show, saying, Can't stick it . . ? What's up with you? Men or what?

Leader moves off from the verge as soon as the pack has caught up because he's already had the chance to gain breath.

'Bastard.'

'Fucking bastard.'

'I fancy a sarnie'

'Me too.'

'Best leave it a couple more miles.'

'Wh've you got?

'Paste. What have you got, you?'

'... Tongue.'

'Swap?'

'Might. Later.'

And the first long climb will lead to the first long descent, one-in-ten, one-in-ten, one-in-ten, each of us says it as we pass the sign, feet off the pedals and the wind rushing, sun in the sky and it's good to be alive.

A front brake fails.

A frayed cable shears, distorted by structural strain. Heels dig in, grind, drag back, scoring the tarmac, turfing lumps out of the soles. WhooahFuck. The back brake's bloody useless, drag the wheel into the kerb and use the tyre as the final buffer – Shit you could get a puncture like this Easy. Everybody laughing, tears streaming, thought you were gonna go arse over tit then, mate, ha ha ha.

Big sigh, check the damage. 'Close. Close one. Got a spanner?'

'Yep, got a combination, but the cable's snapped. Can't do anything with a snapped cable. Need a new one.'

'D'ya think there'll be a shop?'

'Dunno. Sav a look.'

Leader: Come on, leave him with it, if we wait we'll never get there.

'You carry on if you want, we'll fix this.' Look out for your mates. One of our rules.

Leader's authority challenged. The first group split, a faction of three against two in Snapped-cable's favour.

Alright, alright. We'll wait.

Leader and his henchman rest their machines against the green railing which guards the pedestrians from the traffic on the bridge, and they lean over, pivoting on their bellies, spitting into the river below.

Back within the city boundary, a red Lancia pulls up outside a house built of red bricks, lit with cheap metal window frames. A blank front door is painted in one of four colours the council stipulate for front doors. This front door is in council green. The others are yellow, blue, red then green again, and so the sequence repeats, much like the primary shades of children's building blocks. The owner of the red Lancia walks across the neat rectangle of mown grass at the kerb side of the pavement, where the well-mannered dogs generally shit, across the flagged-over part of the pavement where the less well-mannered dogs generally shit, through the gate, across the unmown front lawn – quite large, big enough to take several pieces of abandoned furniture and leave plenty of spare ground – round the side and in through the open back door. He is observed by the neighbour, who sees in his raffish haircut, fancy clothes and shiny shoes incontrovertible evidence of his intentions vis-à-vis Her Nextdoor. She's a sort. The owner of the red Lancia sells cavity wall insulation, but not to these houses. He met Her Nextdoor in a nightclub on a Fridaynight. On this Fridaynight, she won runner-up in a beauty contest they were holding. As she descended from the stage in her sash and swimming costume, he cut in quick, offering her a drink, which she accepted. After a few brandy and Babychams, he took her outside to show her the car he'd been telling her about. The drive they took led to the front bedroom of the house with the green door, passing en route, and quietly, they thought, the back bedroom where the boy with the snapped brake cable slept. The way in which they moved quietly was the way in which people who have been drinking and dancing move quietly. They were fragrant with perfume and had each felt the other's lips hot over their throat and neck, had exhaled into each other's ears, soft and warm; their tongues had already met, and they had been serenaded in the red Lancia by the cassette in the centre console which played the sweet music of José Feliciano. Come On Baby Light My Fire. Into the bedroom with clumsiness and giggles. The room was furnished in the sparest way, and on the bed she quickly and expertly went down on him and quite suddenly he thought he was in love. And the boy with the snapped brake cable, recently asleep, had that sleep disturbed by moans and other noises, and put his head under the pillow. In the morning, the boy watched as the man with the red Lancia gave his mother a few notes; she handed him a blue one. A fiver!

'Get yourself something.'

As it turned out, he was alright, the man with the red Lancia, but the boy with the snapped brake cable knew it wouldn't last.

SCENE 1 INT. KITCHEN. DAY.

HER NEXTDOOR *sits at the unclothed kitchen table wearing a blue dressing gown, her thigh showing where the material falls away. She reads the Daily Mirror. She is smoking.* RED LANCIA *enters through the open back door.*

RED LANCIA: Hi, Babe. On your own?

HER NEXTDOOR: Yeah. (*glances up*) He's out on his bike.

RED LANCIA: (*takes her hand and lights his own from her cigarette*) Nice day for it. And for a bit of the other. What d'ya fancy? (*slips his hand inside the dressing gown*)

HER NEXTDOOR: (*without fondness*) Y' think that's all I'm good for, don't you?

RED LANCIA: Come on. I get here whenever I can . . . You know I'm busy . . .

HER NEXTDOOR: Oh yeah, plenty of cavities to fill . . .

RED LANCIA: Don't be like that. Listen . . . I'll take you away at the weekend . . . Llandudno?

HER NEXTDOOR: Is that a promise?

RED LANCIA: My word is my bond.

Cut to: Brief and perfunctory sex against the kitchen sink. Her Nextdoor pressed against the stainless edge, Red Lancia's trousers in the ludicrous 'round the ankles' position. Both enjoying it.

• ❖ •

City boys are not entirely welcome in the shops at the bottom of the one-in-ten. The shopkeepers are right to be circumspect, because we will steal things. Not brake cables though. We've got a certain unspecifiable respect for cycle shops. The cycle man is a miserable git but he has a cable. Not the right kind, but we buy it anyway (we've all got money, that that we've been given and that that we've stolen from our mums' purses) and soon, by the efforts of our roadside repairs, the bike inverted, re-inverted and inverted once more, we've got the front brake working, because we're specialists, because we spend all our time stealing bikes, building bikes, having bikes stolen from us, stealing bikes and rebuilding bikes. Leader saunters over: Have you fucking finished or what?

Snapped-cable kicks off, pulls a wheelie, turns through a rear-wheel skid (we've tightened that up as well) and grins.

'Yeah. Come on. What you waiting for?'

The next one-in-ten is uphill, and everyone gets off half-way to push. All sweating and panting, and Leader says: I'm gonna be first there. Any bets?

'How much?'

'Quid.'

Sure sure sure we all go, like we'd bet a quid, like we've got it.

'Bet you're not, bet you nothing, just bet you're not.'

He's not gonna win anyway. Can tell you that, because he's riding a long bench seat in lean-back black vinyl with two flags, but with only three gears. He hasn't got a dog's chance.

85

At the top of the second one-in-ten, the land flattens out and the road winds between fields, the fields littered with sheep and cows and boulders, punctuated by drystone walls, farm buildings and tractors. Leader pulls ahead, disappearing round two long bends, dismounts, lays ambush. Pulling the strands of the fence wire wide apart, he slips through the barbs, and in the field picks up a cowpat, the perfect kind, sun-crusted yet soft-centred, and lobs it into the group as they appear, and it cracks in the air and barely misses a direct hit on the *peloton*, breaking sweetly all around as it lands on the ground just ahead.

Right. Fucking right. Get you for that. Bikes abandoned and a cowpat fight is on.

Back within the city boundary, Red Lancia and Her Nextdoor have not had quite enough.

SCENE 2 INT. BEDROOM. DAY.
The bedroom is grim in the daytime light. Drawing the curtains does dampen the harsh glare, but it's not enough to dispel the overwhelming notion that there is little money available round here and hasn't been for years, if ever. There is exotica, however, in the shape of diaphanous garments draped over the dressing-table mirror. Scattered lipstick and hairspray, perfume and make-up litter its surface and the floor. Her Nextdoor sits astride Red Lancia, who is down to an undone shirt and a flailing tie.

RED LANCIA: Ahh . . . ahh . . . ahh . . . ahh . . .

HER NEXTDOOR: Uhh . . . uhh . . . uhh . . . uhh . . .

RED LANCIA: Ahh . . . ahh . . . ahh . . . ahh . . .

HER NEXTDOOR: Uhh . . . uhh . . . uhh . . . uhh . . .

Etc. to Mutual Orgasm. Her Nextdoor lays her body over Red Lancia's, kisses him gently on the cheek.

HER NEXTDOOR: Do you love me?

RED LANCIA: More than anything ever in the history of time.

Her Nextdoor pulls her head back to display a raised eyebrow.

RED LANCIA: On my honour.

The muck-strewn *peloton* rolls into the sleepy market town of Ashbourne in Derbyshire, creating its own sense of debris in the square as it lunches. There is much change and exchange of sarnies, peanut butter for a banana and honey, tongue for a jam, paste for a cheese and pickle. The bread is peeled back, the contents examined and garnished with crisps and broken biscuits, squashed together again and gobbled with relish, but without lashings of ginger beer. When the food's all gone, the group pool their funds and buy two pounds of cherries from a stall. It's market day. The stallholder is another miserable git. A stone-spitting contest ends in a cherry-throwing decider. Three consecutive hits on the hotel sign clinch it. Jubilation.

Discussing the exact nature of each other's most aching part – arses compete with thighs for this – the *peloton* reassembles, climbs out of the sleepy town, aiming towards the stepping stones which ford the river at Dovedale. Gnats frost our hair like icing sugar on a mince tart.

A red Lancia with the hood pulled down glides through the city, occasionally stalling at the lights. Her Nextdoor is at the wheel. He avoids driving in the daytime if he can help it, because he's banned and rather well-known. He lights up two Bensons and hands one over, laughing nervously, afraid, most mortally afraid that the car will be pranged up, and offers a huge amount of advice aimed at avoiding such an outcome. Advice which she could do without. She's not listening to it anyway, she's having a think, working out how to play it when they get to the office. Catching sight of a bobby on the beat he yells out, All Coppers Are Bastards, and ducks down chuckling. Fuckin 'ell, Babe, she says, well alarmed.

SCENE 3 INT. AN OFFICE IN THE CITY CENTRE. DAY.
They arrive at Red Lancia's place of work, parking on a dirt patch behind the tiny isolated building. Entering through a door coated with peeling off-white paint, they find his partner, FAT SALOON, *lounging behind a brown counter, feet on it. Behind Fat Saloon a chart hangs on the wall, showing the names of the sales force and their hits this week and to date. It's like a league table, an indicator of performance. There are few players in this league.*

FAT SALOON: Alright, how's tricks?
RED LANCIA: Gonna take some time off. Me and Cheryl

are gonna go to the country. Weather's too good to miss.

CHERYL: (*sits on counter top and strokes Fat Saloon's hair*) Alright, Honey? We need to spend some time together, you know. I think I could be good for him.

FAT SALOON: Doing a bit of work'd be good for him.

RED LANCIA: Not exactly the best of weather for cavity wall, is it? I've been thinking . . . we should branch out. Exterior coatings are coming in. Gonna be big. You know the stuff, decorative, like pebbledash sort of thing. They call it Tyrolean. They've got a new spray-on system. Nigel Gilligham's doing it.

FAT SALOON: So I've heard.

CHERYL: Any chance of a cup of tea? . . . I'll do 'em. Sugars?

RED LANCIA: Three please, Babe.

Fat Saloon rattles a plastic container of Hermesetas. Red Lancia gets on the phone:

RED LANCIA: Yeah, your coatings, the wife picked up a leaflet, she's going on about how good it'd look on our place but I said I'm not having anybody round without like an idea, y'know. What sort of price is it? Yeah . . . three-bed semi. Ooh bloody hell . . . that sounds a bit steep. I'll get back to you. Bye. (*turns to Fat Saloon*) Idiot gave me a price just like that. Must be new. Two grand! We could do with some of that.

FAT SALOON: (*to Cheryl*) Full of it, isn't he?

CHERYL: He was.

Red Lancia laughs and puts his hand up Cheryl's skirt. She squirms free.

CHERYL: Haven't you ever had enough?

RED LANCIA: Where's that tea?

FAT SALOON: (*sighs*) You want to put a bit of bromide in it. Best you two do clear off, you're making me feel ill. Maybe catch you in The Feathers later. About eight?

The red Lancia moves out into the countryside, switching past motor showrooms and petrol stations, switching past the remand centre, switching beside the slaughterhouses at Cellarhead and into Real Country, switches into argument:

SCENE 4 EXT. CAR ON ROAD. DAY.

RED LANCIA: I'll drive now. Pull over.

CHERYL: Oh, can't I carry on? I'm enjoying meself.

RED LANCIA: It's dangerous for women to drive on country roads. I wanna give it some clog anyway.

Cheryl emergency stops, squealing wheels.

RED LANCIA: Fuck! Trying to do? Get us killed?

Cheryl climbs over the driver's door – with the window down it's a low hurdle easily straddled – stands, hands on hips, in the middle of the road. Red Lancia, despite himself, gives a moment's pause to admire the way the sun makes her skirt transparent, the crotch beautifully silhouetted. He slides into the driving seat; Cheryl moves with her finest catwalk strut, rounds the bonnet and lowers herself into the passenger side, staring straight ahead, aloof. Red Lancia grinds the gear, skids the rear wheels, leaving behind a print on the tarmac like a fossil pattern in a rock stratum.

The *peloton*, now on foot, pushes along beside the river sucking in unison on plastic bottles, the bottles filled with clear water which was discovered spurting from inside the earth. Spring water tastes good, cold. The valley is disarmingly hushed, the river is wide here and flows steadily, the ripple as the spume cuts round the rocks plays at pianissimo, a volume at odds with the city rumble which forms the normal soundtrack to our lives. An echo effect is created by the hills, which pitch up from each bank at a gradient greater than one-in-ten. So the hush is magnified, reflected from sun-dried grass and white shale, filtered through the leaves on the trees to hang in a druggy haze over the river.

The car bucks through the country roads, gearing down into the bends, kicking away whining. Wind streaming through Cheryl's hair ripples like a Bardot movie still, Red Lancia's rolling slick like an ad in a hair salon. Blood Sweat and Tears through the speakers – God Bless The Child. Cheryl softens, strokes his thigh. Some days it's good to be alive.

The stepping stones are strung across the river at the widest point, flat-topped, mirage marshmallow pillows, rising solid. On Bank Holidays there's a queue. Someone always falls in. The river runs cold, sudden immersion takes our breath away. Come up gasping.

Today it's quiet. Bikes dropped to the ground, pedals knocking up dust on the underside, wheels spinning and clicking, the *pelotonniers* dance across the water singing: We won the war in Nineteen Forty-Four, We won the war in Nineteen Forty-Four.

The group separates into its earlier formation, and from each side staves are found to fight the crossing. Robin Hood v Little John. Us against the Germans. Whatever. Each of us says to himself, I won't fall in, not me. Everybody does.

Clothes drying over rocks on the bank. Five milky bodies flat out, eyes looking as near to the sun as possible, closed tight and opened quickly, making pixillations. Leader boasts of his sex life. Two fingers up Karen Swift. A couple of us prop our heads on our hands at this, examine Leader's face to assess whether or not it might be true. The possibility it is true has us wondering how we might next speak to Karen Swift. Abuse or ingratiation. Snapped-cable lies the stillest. The river continues gentle, its quietness a rhythm, and Leader breaks the air once more: Our Neil says anyone can have your mum.

Snapped-cable stays on his back pretending he didn't hear; but the red flashing into his face tells another story. Heads propped higher on hands focus on Leader, waiting to see if he'll repeat it. Leader and Snapped-cable live near enough to each other. Leader could know. We're all thinking it might be true anyway; actually, it could be true. Those of us who know how to feel sorry for people feel sorry for Snapped-cable. His dad fucked off a while back, though that was not a bad thing. You can't keep it a secret when that happens cos of the free school meals.

Yeah, says Leader, Neil told me Michael Mitchell said he's been there. Good ride, your mum.

Snapped-cable cracks, comes out of the blocks at Leader, fingernails groove straight into his flaccid front, knees rucking at his stomach ribs, but Leader's bigger, stronger, meaner and turns Snapped-cable on his back. He sits astride him, pulls his arms apart in the full crucifixion position and pins the limbs under his knees, straightens his spine, tilts his head back and sniffs up some gobbit, rolls it in his mouth and lets it go slow, landing it on Snapped-cable's closed eyelid. The gob flecks off his cheek as he whips his head trying to clear it, tears running and calling out GettoffyouBastardfuckingBastardGettoff. We've seen enough and tell Leader. Leave him alone Come on Get off him Leave him alone. But he continues to pin Snapped-cable and humiliate him a while longer before our disapprobation works. If it ever does. Maybe he just gets bored and finishes in his own time, the time it would have taken anyway. Leader affects hurt, Look what he's fucking done, he says, pointing to the weals rising. Shuttup. We all say it except Snapped-cable who says nothing.

SCENE 5 EXT. PUB CAR PARK IN THE COUNTRY. LATE AFTERNOON.
Cheryl and Red Lancia rest against the red Lancia admiring the view.

RED LANCIA: Great view.

CHERYL: Mmm!

RED LANCIA: We used to have some fun out here when I was a boy.

CHERYL: (*lights two Bensons, hands him one*) Don't you have fun any more, then?

Red Lancia hesitates. He'd really prefer that there were no lipstick on the filter. He draws on the cigarette, sips on his beer, foam garnishing his moustache. He puts his arm round Cheryl's waist, spooning her to him.

RED LANCIA: Different sorts of fun when you grow up, aren't there?

Cheryl giggles, Red Lancia nuzzles her neck.

RED LANCIA: I'll let you into a secret.

CHERYL: Go on.

RED LANCIA: Boys never grow up.

CHERYL: Call that a secret?

Cheryl slips her hand down his trousers.

CHERYL: Some parts grow though, don't they?

RED LANCIA: Oh yeah. Some parts grow.

The *peloton* presses further up the valley. Snapped-cable elects to stay put, sits with his back to a tree sucking on a blade of grass.

'Come on, we've said don't let him spoil it, stay with us.'

I'm stopping here. Cos that's what I want to do, that's why. Leave it. Just leave it, will you?

We leave it.

About an hour further upstream is as far as we go, then we turn back, rolling down the thin, worn path, standing on the pedals, squeezing the brakes, cruising sidesaddle. There might be time to make it back before it's dark. The rolling path flattens out to a wide meadow and we swing ourselves into our seats, bumping over the easy cobble of grass. Ahead Snapped-cable can be seen slowly negotiating the stepping stones, arms outstretched for balance, shakily moving from one bank to the other. He spots us in the distraction we make lifting our bikes over the stile, stops mid-river and steps deliberately down into the water, stands still and stares, wades to the bank. D'you wanna get a rash then? Leader nods at the sodden trousers. Snapped-cable says nothing, picking up his bike, setting off in the lead.

The return journey is tatty, the *peloton* stretched out, losing coherence. The expectation gone, the food gone, limbs genuinely aching, the light failing, the temperature dropping; miles seem longer. Snapped-cable pulls ahead, fuelled, looking to climb the first reverse one-in-ten without rising out of the saddle. When he succumbs, he stands on the pedals, legs pumping, body rolling, refusing the desire to get off and push. Leader is struggling, the long bench seat in lean-back black vinyl with two flags but with only three gears is not the machine for reverse one-in-tens. He's gone quiet. Thunder rumbles for a long polluted drag as an articulated truck strains against the incline, keeping us company for too long, dust and chicken feathers from its cargo peppering our faces and our forearms, diesel fumes clogging us in the afterdraught. As the air clears, there's no sight of Snapped-cable. At the top, the diminishing truck is all the movement we can see away down the long straight.

SCENE 6 EXT. CAR ON ROAD. EARLY EVENING.
The red Lancia pulls out of the pub car park into the road, cutting up another driver, who flashes his lights. Cheryl turns and blows the driver a kiss.

RED LANCIA: Nice one.

Red Lancia drops the accelerator, checking the mirror as the flashing lights recede in the distance, clocking the rising speedo needle. They're flying now.

CHERYL: Whoah. I love this.
RED LANCIA: Yeah. Metal to the pedal. Put the metal to the pedal.

Red Lancia overtakes a tractor slalom-style, like he was playing a games machine, one hand on the wheel, Cheryl inclining into his shoulder, his free arm around her.

CHERYL: Like being in the driving seat, don't you?
RED LANCIA: I like being in any position, me.

Forearms rested low on the handlebars, guiding not steering, lungs pulsing, heart marking a regular beat. On my own now On my own now On my own. Chain clicks through the derailleur, lollipop stick long discarded.

Chaff chaff chaff, the rhythm as the rim brushes the brake block, identifying the buckle once per revolution. Thighs burning, head hanging, eyes on the ground, the panning tarmac mesmerizing and cohesive; it used to happen to the sky when you were twizzed when you were little. Forearms rested low on the handlebars, guiding not steering.

A front brake fails. Shit. It never lasts if you fix it with the wrong sort. Snapped-cable dismounts, ties the twine round the lever, glances back, remounts and continues.

◆ ❖ ◆

SCENE 7 EXT. LAY-BY. DUSK.

RED LANCIA: Mmm . . . Mmm . . . Mmm . . . Mmm . . .
CHERYL: Huh . . . Huh . . . Huh . . . Huh . . .
RED LANCIA: Mmm . . . Mmm . . . Mmm . . . Mmm . . .
CHERYL: Huh . . . Huh . . . Huh . . . Huh . . .

The two figures rise, flushed. Smiling.

CHERYL: I'm hungry.
RED LANCIA: Hungry?
CHERYL: Yeah. Hungry.
RED LANCIA: Chinese?
CHERYL: Mmm.

The red Lancia eases into the carriageway.

◆ ❖ ◆

All the way down the penultimate one-in-ten, Snapped-cable is braking with his feet, simultaneously pulling on the semi-efficient back brake. The last fast straight runs to the traffic lights by the bridge; he skews the front wheel awkwardly to bring the machine to a halt, finding the thin spot and busting the inner tube. Shit. He turns the bike on the pavement and starts levering the tyre. By the time the middle section of the *peloton* arrives, he's drying the residual glue with chalk powder, grating the cube against the tin. All pull to the kerb.

'D'you get a puncture?'

'What do you think?'

'Brake gone again?'

He glances at the frayed twine.

'D'you want us to wait?'

'No. I'll catch you anyway. Where's that twat?'

'Dunno, we left him about four mile back. His bike's shit.'

SCENE 8 EXT. CAR ON ROAD. LATE DUSK.
The sky bleeding blue, rising red, the city outline parabolic on the horizon. The occupants quiet, sunglasses on. The car drifts towards the lights, travelling along the road which runs square to the one-in-ten.

Teasing the repaired tube back into the tyre, he hears the fat-spreading rubber hum of Leader's tyres. He continues to work, preoccupied. Leader pulls up.

'Got a problem?'

Nothing.

'Puncture. Want to get some decent tyres.'

Nothing.

Leader lights up a Number Ten. Blows the smoke with extravagance.

'I meant it, y'know. I'm not taking it back what I said.'

'You're a cunt anyway.' Without raising his head, twisting the adaptor into the pump.

Leader coughs smoke. 'Say that again.'

Snapped-cable begins pumping, muttering low the line once more.

Leader props his bike on its stand. Moves forward.

SCENE 9 EXT. CAR STOPPED AT LIGHTS. LATE LATE DUSK.
Red Lancia leans, kisses Cheryl on the lips. Over her shoulder, an altercation between two boys draws his eye.

RED LANCIA: That's not your lad over there, is it?

Cheryl follows his gaze.

CHERYL: It is too. He's got one of those Wilkinsons with him. A right shower they are.

RED LANCIA: Are they scrappin'?

Leader has pulled his face to within inches of Snapped-cable's to make the request: Say it again, go on, I dare you. Say it again.

RED LANCIA: Oyy!

Snapped-cable grips the pump. You're an ugly fucking cunt. Leader seizes Snapped-cable by the throat.

RED LANCIA: Oyy!

Snapped-cable prods the pump into Leader's guts with one hand, mauling him away with the other.

RED LANCIA: Oyyy!

Snapped-cable and Leader turn to see what all the commotion's about.

RED LANCIA: D'you wanna lift?
SNAPPED-CABLE: What about me bike?
RED LANCIA: Stick it in the back.
SNAPPED-CABLE: Alright then.

Snapped-cable turns to Leader.

SNAPPED-CABLE: Nice car, eh?

Leader says nothing.

◆ ❖ ◆

As the red Lancia re-enters the city boundary, it passes what's left of the *peloton*. Snapped-cable sits up on the boot, feet on the narrow back seat, cradling the vertically protruding front wheel of his bike in one arm. The *pelotonniers* call out and wave. Snapped-cable remains impassive.

'Lucky bastard.'

'Nice car . . .'

Laughter.

◆ ❖ ◆

SCENE 10 INT. CHINESE RESTAURANT. NIGHTFALL.
Waiter taking order at table.

WAITER: . . . Two number three. And the young man?

CHERYL: Have you decided yet?

SNAPPED-CABLE: Thirty-nine.

CHERYL: Sweet and Sour?

SNAPPED-CABLE: Yeah.

CHERYL: Nice end to the day for you, isn't it?

SNAPPED-CABLE: Yeah.

RED LANCIA: Listen. I want to ask you something. Can I take your mum away at the weekend? Would you be alright on your own?

CHERYL: Course he will, won't you?

SNAPPED-CABLE: Yeah. I'll be fine.

Cheryl and Red Lancia hold hands across the table. Snapped-cable parades his fingers over a chopstick, a tightrope-walker, tracing the inscribed pattern of incomprehensible script back and forth, back and forth, back and forth.

END

Yeah!

'Are you frightened?'
'A bit. Are you?'
'Yeah. A bit. Does it hurt?'
'A bit. Yes.'
'Be there soon.'
'Yes.'

Not too bad, the traffic. Could be worse. Be there soon.

'Stay seated. I'll come round your side. Is the bag in the
    boot?'
'Yes. Should be. That's where you packed it.'
'This is the right entrance, isn't it?'
'You are hopeless . . . Yes.'
'Thought so. Sorry.'
'Oof.'

The lift. Over there. It's not far.

'Fourth floor?'
'Yes.'
'The lift's alright? It won't make your tummy go
    funny?'
'Do want me to walk? Up the stairs?'

'Sorry . . . So where do we go now? One of these side
    rooms?'
'Ask the nurse.'

They could do with a coat of paint, these corridors. It's all
peeling.

'Have her waters broken?'
'Yeah. Yes.'
'OK honey, let's have a look at you. Lie down. We'll see if
    there's a delivery room free. How often are the con-
    tractions?'
'About every fifteen minutes.'
'Good. That's good.'
'Hold my hand.'

Warm hand. Yellow line. Gonna get a ticket. Bugger. Forgot the tape. Birthing music. Talking Heads mostly.

'Your hand's warm.'
'Yours is cold.'
'Wonder how long it'll take?'
'Sooner the better. Just hope it's alright.'
'Yeah. Course it will be.'
'I love you, y'know.'

Yeah. I love you too, y'know.

'I never thought it'd be like buses.'
'What d'you mean?'
'All this waiting around. Nothing happening.'

'Oh yes, it's just like buses. Huh. Triplets in here.'
'Better get back to Mothercare. Buy more cots. Huh.'
'Ow. Ahh. Ahhh. I think something's coming . . .'

When they had that show-you-round-the-thing at the hospital one of them fainted when we came in the theatre. It is a bit clinical.

'Come on honey, one more push, come on, one big one . . .'
'Jesus. I can see the head.'
'That's it, one more . . .'
'Ahhhhhhhh.'
'There. Beautiful boy. You're a big one, aren't you?'
'Hello. Beautiful baby.'

Looks slimy. Covered in blood and stuff. Jesus.

'They're doing the weighing-him thing. You alright?'
'Yes. Yes. I am now. We did it!'
'We did it. You did it. You did well.'
'Isn't he beautiful?'
'Yeah. He sure is, man.'
'Waaahh!'

Noisy. That boy is a noisy baby.

'Right. We can get you to the ward now.'
'Did you like being wheeled on a trolley? Size of your tits. Plenty in there for him, eh?'
'Mmm. 'S nice. Feeding feels nice.'

'Shall I go now? Call everybody?'
'Yes. The list's by the phone. My mum first, remember?'
'Yeah. Sure. Bye son. Bye baby. Kiss.'

Ticket. Knew it. Bugger.

'Nine and a half pounds. Yeah.'
'Yeah. Nine and a half pounds.'
'Nine and a half pounds.'
'Nine and a half pounds.'
'Nine and a half pounds.'
'Yeah, the nurse said he was a big one. Last orders? Yeah!'

The world is a wonderful place.

Ice-Cubes

She was sitting playing with her hair scrunchy, rolling it round and round her hands and wrists, the long denim dress she was wearing tucked under her feet on the chair. She was telling me about the night she and Jim spent trying to fix up a cot for their baby. Neither of them was at all practical, and about half-way through the cot fixing she'd got fed up, picked up a fabric dice and rolled it to the child. It was one of those big dice, she said, a soft red cube with white and blue dots. She couldn't remember which number came up. She laughed when she said that, but without smiling. Jim had turned on her and, slow and measured, said, I suppose you think that'll help, do you? She said she just looked at him, and she wanted the look to say, Come on, this is hard enough, this baby and all, without you starting, please don't start, not now. Jim, he might have seen that in her eyes, but he was tired; more than anything at all he was tired. The baby didn't sleep. Jim hated waking in the night. He'd been having his sleep interrupted for six months now and it was screwing his system right up. The waking, the getting of his eyes open, felt, he struggled to find an expression which would convey it, it felt like maybe forcing a tyre off a rim. You know when you watch the guys do that at the tyre shop – the slow wrench which sees the rubber part from the steel?

That was kind of how it was for him to open his eyes. And probably because of the weight of his tiredness, Jim didn't see all those things she said were in her eyes. Crouching, he sort of looked through her, to the baby in the corner, slung low in one of those baby holders they'd got all over the place now, this one the little deck chair with a row of rattling things dangling across the front of it. The baby was making clumsy swipes at them. On the floor around him Jim tracked the pieces of cot: dowels of pine, steel rods, plastic lugs, a sheet of cardboard; an instruction leaflet in eight languages. Fixing the cot had got to the point where he didn't know which bit was which any more. He watched the dice roll to the baby. The baby clutched it and raised it, and tried to force the corner into its mouth, but the corner was too big so the baby dribbled over the dice, a thin bubbling stream of baby-gurgle soaking the cube. She said that she watched Jim rise, slowly gaze around him, and she knew what he could see. Everywhere he looked he saw baby stuff, or stuff that was hers but was baby-related, like the underwear on the radiator. You know, the radiators just have underwear on them the whole time now, he said. That was all he said. And he stood there, and he knew it was too much for him, that he couldn't put the cot together, that the flat was taken over by baby stuff, that he couldn't sleep properly any more, that he wasn't making enough money to keep things afloat, though God knows he worked hard enough and took on every job that came along, that he'd even got his father working for him now, for Christsakes. And instead of seeing the baby, who he knew he loved or anyway she knew he loved, he definitely did, and her, he loved her still she thought, he still wanted to make love to her any-way; instead of seeing any love and a way forward out of it, he just saw a problem that would never go away. She watched as he stepped over to the baby, leant down to pull the dice from its mouth. The baby had two teeth, the front two at the top had come through, and as he pulled at the dice with a sudden vicious motion, the fabric tore on the baby's tooth. That little tearing sound ripped through her head, amplified a hundred times, because she felt it coming, she'd felt it coming for a while now, she knew deep down inside her that Jim had been getting closer to the edge. She hadn't wanted to admit it to herself. She didn't look at Jim, she put herself between him and the baby, her back to Jim, and she cradled the child in her arms, picked it up and rocked it gently against her shoul-der. Jesus. That was all Jim said. He clattered about in the hall: the jangle of his keys, the scuffing of his jacket along the wall, the door shutting gently behind him.

Outside, he leans back against the door, rubs his head against the knocker, giving his skull a primitive massage. He knows what's up. She was over-protective. He'd tell her later. As if he'd ever hurt the baby. He'd never hurt the baby. He climbs the steps, steep steps rise from the basement in which they live, ascending to the street. He heads towards Charlie's, round the corner, past the back of the station. Charlie is cool and will give him something to smoke. He buys a four-pack from the off-licence on the way, so he has something to offer in exchange. He makes his way down to Charlie's door, Charlie has a basement flat too. He knocks. The window-shutter shifts slightly, a moment later Charlie opens the door, lets him in. Charlie's place is like a building site, he has work-benches all over the place. It always smells of timber down here, sappy new timber, and sweet dope smoke. Charlie is quite beautiful, a skinny dread who smokes all day long. They settle into Charlie's room, the basecamp room in which he lives. Charlie's world is in here, the bed, the HiFi, the TV, and Charlie's secret underfloor hiding places for drugs and money. Charlie makes a spliff, Jim cracks open two cans and they chew the fat like good old boys, Jim telling of domestic problems, Charlie offering the benefit of his experience.

The baby was grouching and whingeing, she wondered whether to phone the doctor. She said she didn't like to bother the doctor after a certain time of night. She paced up and down the hall, the baby's head resting against her as she patted and rubbed its back. The child wouldn't be soothed, its little head reared back, its face purple with misery and sodden with tears. There, there, there, she said, There now. Hush, hush. But the baby wouldn't hush. The baby was letting out yowls which echoed from the walls. It echoed louder when it was just her and the baby. She lay down on the bed and opened her shirt, undid the clasp at the front of her bra. For a few minutes the baby was comforted. She lay there breathing deeply, regularly. Everything stilled, she said. Silence dropped like snow.

Charlie chops out two lines of coke. With a Stanley blade, on a bathroom mirror placed on a Workmate, he lays out parallel a pair of sparkling welts. Charlie wipes the fine white excess dust from the glass with his forefinger, which he cleans with his tongue, the powder fizzing like sherbet. As Jim hoovers the line up his nose using a rolled twenty, he studies his close-up in the mirror. The vessels around his nose look shot; rising grey, then fading, the colour in the bags under his eyes runs away to a milkiness, a rim of mottled verdigris defining the perimeter of the lids. His pupils are large but empty, reflecting nothing. He pulls his head back and sniffs hard, the powder scours his right nostril. Charlie follows suit. Their eyes meet, glistening with expectancy, waiting for the hit. It takes about a minute. Charlie is a connoisseur who prides himself on handling only high-quality stuff. They continue chewing the fat like old boys on coke; which is to say they chew faster, louder and more lucidly, or so it seems to them.

The baby had pulled away from her breast suddenly, gurgling and choking, and let out several hiccups of milky sick. The thin stench rose to her nostrils. Poor baby, she said. She mopped the spew up with a muslin square, moved the baby to the little carrycot, the one for which it was getting too big, and went to the bathroom to rinse the muslin out under the tap. She pulled the cord on the shaver light, wincing as she examined her features. I looked at her then, as she told me how she thought she could see right through herself, how her skin had gone so thin and colourless, she felt like it was holding nothing in, like there was nothing inside. Her features were pale and delicate, everything about her was fine, her nose was slim with freckles placed just-so, her ears were turned small, the lobes like milkdrops. She pulled her hair back behind her, twisting it into a knot. What she said, how she saw herself, I could imagine her feeling that she looked that way. It was easy to picture.

She rested her forehead on the mirror, the surface was cold and felt nice, soothing. The baby began to cry again and she had the idea that it too might feel better if it had something cold against its forehead like that; it would be nice for the baby to feel like she was feeling now with the mirror pressed against her face. She said she rolled her cheek onto the mirror until the surface misted, that it felt really good. She took the muslin square to the kitchen, opened the freezer box at the top of the fridge, laid the muslin over the table and tapped the ice-cube tray out onto it. The kitchen had a concrete floor, painted red, she said, and she half-smiled then. She stooped down and hammered the muslin onto the floor, holding it like a slingshot, swinging it over her head onto the deck to crush the ice, so that it would shape easily over the baby's head. She said it was such a release, like hitting somebody only better, because nobody got hurt. Flecks of water spat out from the muslin, scattering against the skirting and the dirty bases of the appliances.

Jim leaves Charlie's suddenly. They've had more dope, more coke, and Jim is feeling unwell. His heart is beating like crazy, his brain is hot. It's called a rush. You alright, man? asks Charlie. Yeah, just need some air. Jim walks round and round the block, trying to restore equilibrium, thinking a normal activity like walking will do it. It's not working, waves of panic and frantic heart-beating wash over him. He increases the size of the block, walking right round the edge of the park; he thinks, Don't die now, not like this, what will everybody think – He died of an overdose and left the baby, poor baby, so small.

She cradled the muslin-wrapped ice in her hand, a delicious cold stream leaked over her wrist, running to the crease in her elbow. The lock sounded and Jim entered, looking whiter than she'd ever seen him before. Are you OK? she asked. Jim shook his head. Lie down, she said, Lie by the baby. And he lay dislocated on the floor beside the carrycot, and held the baby's hand, tiny and precious, in his own clammy palm. She placed the pack of ice delicately over his forehead. Jim reached to his side and picked the dice off the floor, inserting a finger into the little tear. Sorry. That was all he said.

Off the Plot

Soon after Jamie was born I lost my job. Jamie was our first child. He overwhelmed me, so tiny, so beautiful. The responsibility of caring for him pressed in on me, like I was deep under water. I worked in software. One Friday some madness hit me. I told the boss where to shove it. The firm was one of those small businesses with bad cash-flow. I'd done about forty hours overtime that month, but it never turned up on my salary slip. It wasn't the first time this had happened. I blew my top with him, swore at him. I suppose I threw the job away more than I lost it. It made me feel good though, letting that cocksucker know my true feelings. I knew there would be no reference coming after that. I left right then, at lunchtime, seething all the way back home, walking hard, feeling angry but free at the same time. I picked up the local paper, ran water into a glass, and sat on the edge of the fire surround in the lounge, going through the small job ads. The small small job ads. The non-display ads. I wasn't looking forward to telling Mandy what I'd done, she'd crack up. I searched through jobs for which you wouldn't need a reference. Telesales? The thought made me shudder. Bar work? Big money. Earn over 25K, no experience necessary. Yeah. Sure.

There were plenty for Owner Drivers. One thing I had

going for me, one piece of machinery I could regard as plant and equipment, was the car. We have an old Mercedes saloon, midnight blue, with black leather seats. It's got well over a hundred thousand on the clock. We really love that car. We go to the coast in it some weekends, drive home late, when the motorway seems wider, when it's dark and quiet. It hugs the road, fat and comfortable and safe. The first number I called was the ad which was briefest: Owner Drivers, Top Circuit. The guy who answered the phone didn't speak to me straight off. I could hear him in the background talking over the air, Bittersea, zero four, B-i-t-t-e-r-s-e-a, he was saying, Roger, zero four, roger, Rog. Give us a POB when you've got them, yeah. Rog. He came back to me and said, Sorry. Relay Cars. Where to? His voice was big and gentle, slightly lispy. I told him I was calling about the advert in the paper. Okay-dokay, he said, Can you start tonight? I'm a bit pushed.

I wanted to say no, that I had plans, that it was inconvenient, even though I didn't, even though it wasn't. Shit, I was thinking, this is a new market. No application-interview-wait-for-the-letter-hand-in-notice-farewell-drink. He doesn't even need to meet me. Come over about six, I'll get someone to sort you a radio, he says. Ask for Dean. I'll be here in the office anyway. Alright?

OK is all I can think of to say in reply.

Mandy was out. This was the time of day she'd walk Jamie in the park. I sat waiting, running my finger through the dust on the grate. She came in through the back door, startled to find me there. I told her what had happened. She looked gutted. Hollowness her eyes flooded with.

Which made me sad and angry and it made me want to cry at the same time. Her lip trembled. I held her close. Maybe I did. I tried to reassure her, saying, You know, I'm getting straight back out, earning again. We'll Be Alright. Career-wise, though, this was undoubtedly a move in the wrong direction. We both knew that.

A regular-looking bloke with wavy ginger hair fitted up the radio. Tony. He was the company mechanic. He was the kind of mechanic who was unqualified and not very good, anyone could see that at a glance. It only took him about ten minutes to get the radio fitted though, he wired it straight onto the battery, through the head-lining. We tucked it under the seat. I opened the ashtray and hung the mouthset from it. I kneeled on the pavement, fiddling with the buttons on the set checking for volume and tone, establishing a contact with the office, trying out my call sign, zero eight, while Tony passed the aerial lead under the well-mats, behind the backrest of the rear seat and fed the cable up through the boot. The aerial base was attached magnetically to the rear wing. That was our car, ready to go. Even by the end of that first night it didn't feel like ours any more.

I started with a pick-up from base, to a pub, and I didn't stop for hours. Job came on job came on job. I was lost half the time, driving with an A-Z in one hand and half an eye on the road. Sometimes it was hard to catch what they were saying over the air. I got into parts of town I'd never known before, had people in the car that nor-mally I'd only observe from a distance. They were the kind of people who unnerved me. There were girls who offered things other than cash for the fare. I didn't believe them, I thought they were just winding me up. To tell you what some of the guys were like – one had a tattoo round his neck, a perforated line with CUT HERE written at the front of his throat. I expected to be attacked half the time.

I found, though, a kind of comfort in the voice carrying through the ether, it kept me calm, made me feel like I was attached to something. In the middle of the night, about three-thirty, when it went completely quiet, Dean put out a call to all cars saying that zero two was checking into the twenty-four-hour chicken place, what did we all want. We put in our orders, rendezvoused at base, and I met the boys. They all looked totally shagged, blue-ringed eyes, shot skin. It was a future that might have been mine. They smoked, ate and drank simultaneously. I sat in the corner on the sofa, which was an old rear seat from a Ford Anglia, and listened to the conversation, joining in a bit, using the same slurring, glottal voice pattern that they all used, like something they'd seen or heard on a film. After a while Dean left to get a few hours' sleep. He took his dog with him, a Rottweiler called Führer. Führer had been moving lazily about, scavenging bones. Zero two took over as controller.

By five a.m. things were busying up and I was on the road once more. I took a family to the airport, which was about thirty miles away. This was a coveted job, an earner. The family had picked up a standby flight, they told me. The grown-ups were on their best behaviour, being nice with each other in a way that felt as though it must be unusual, like they were at a wedding or something. The children were all keyed-up, a little irritating. After I'd got their bags out and they'd paid me, when they were out of sight, I parked and walked into the main building across the concourse. Through the picture window overlooking the runways I watched one plane land and one take off. Such a weight to move around. On the way back I radioed that I was clocking off the plot.

When I got home it was midday. I'd been driving for about sixteen hours. Feeling light-headed through lack of sleep, I crashed out almost immediately after briefing Mandy, giving an edited version of the night's events. I had a hundred and twenty pounds in coins and notes in my jacket pocket. I slept, woke feeling terrible, and did the same thing all over again on Saturday night and Sunday morning. That one weekend I earned more than two weeks' salary at the software place after deductions. I was hooked. I actually liked it. I liked being in motion in the middle of the night, when the skyline ached, drenched in blueblack, when the roads were marked out just for me. I liked having a call number. I liked it that I was known by this different name, it was like having another identity, a second signature. When I got in in the mornings, I'd say to Jamie, Hi there, zero one, tickling him under the chin. Remember me? It's your dad – zero eight. Mandy didn't like me talking to him this way. She didn't like the implication in the word zero. And she didn't like it that I was out most nights and sleeping during the day. The money though – we were no worse off than before. After a few weeks, Mandy thought we were doing well enough to raise another loan. Maybe get off on holiday.

Dean started to become friendly with me. Dean was from India. He was big-boned, solid. Führer and he were one of those owner-looks-like-the-dog combinations. He'd got Roy's, the café next door, to start selling samosas. I'd pull in to base and pick up a couple when things went quiet. Personally, I trusted the vegetarian ones more than the meat ones. We'd eat them with the lime pickle he kept under the counter and we'd talk.

All sorts come through here, he said. People studying, like zero five. He's training to be a social worker, you know.

Yeah, I said, I've talked to him.

'Basket cases like the professor [zero six]. People who just are cab drivers, like zero nine. Drifters like zero two.'

And me? I said. He looked at me. He'd got soft dark eyes, like Führer.

'You haven't decided what you're doing yet. You're between things. You'll work it out.'

At that moment I felt like Dean was offering me a beat-ification. Very Zen.

I crossed the road and picked up a coffee. A new Seven-Eleven store had opened up. An American import. It was a well-chosen site. Our drivers gave them stacks of business. They had a microwave you could use yourself, if you fancied a disgusting sausage roll or something similar. It didn't last long, the break-dancers who used to congregate outside enjoyed chucking foil trays into it, setting off the fireworks.

Back in the car, I picked up my book from the dash, burning my tongue with the drink, and read while I waited for a job to come in. I was rereading The Catcher in the Rye, a book a friend passed on to me when we were at college. Do you know it? It's brilliant. Dead funny. It's about an American high-schooler, Holden Caulfield, who's a serial flunker and expellé. Mostly he flunks out just for being arsey. Arsey in a hopeless sort of way. He can't work the world out, he thinks grown-ups are all jerks. The book captures a night or two in his life, when he has to make his way home to his folks in New York, to tell them he's flunked again. It's about the journey he has on the way, that and his commentary on life around him, about the jerks he meets. Near the end he sneaks into his little sister's room, back at his parents' place, in the middle of the night. He loves his little sister, who's cool and much brighter than he is, and he tells her that the only thing he wants to be is a catcher in the rye. Like if there were a big field of rye near a cliff edge, with children playing in it, whirling about and so on, and he was the only person around who wasn't a child, he would stop them from falling over the edge, like an angel: be a catcher in the rye. The hanging about side of cab-driving is good for reading.

One Tuesday night, I'm sitting on the plot, getting near to the end of the book, when I hear a new controller on the air. A woman's voice, smoked and nice. The first job falls to zero three. All drivers can hear the controller, but not each other. He must be trying it on a bit, she's pretty short with him. Zero six gets the next one. I can tell from her end that he's trying to chat her up too. There's a little smile in her voice as she bats him off. I speed through the book's final pages, hoping to finish before my fare comes up. In the last lines Holden says he kind of misses everybody he's talked about. Even the total bastards.

Don't ever tell anybody anything. If you do, you start missing everybody.

That's the absolute last line. I'd completely forgotten it from the first time.

'Zero eight.'

I press the button on the handset.

– Yeah. Zero eight. It's my normal response.

She gives me a pick-up from the station, going local. I don't say much, just do the job. Then a few more. I collect a couple from base at closing time; I don't go in, but I stretch in my seat to see her through the window. She's just a smeared silhouette, the window's filthy. At about one, I clock off the plot. Tuesdays are slow. I'm getting a bit more sleep in the week now. Most of my earning's done over the weekend. At home, I let myself in quietly. They're both asleep. The boy's in our bed. His forehead coats with a fine perspiration when he sleeps. I don't want to disturb them so I just lie down on the floor, cover myself with the spare duvet.

One early morning at quarter to seven I take the new night controller home at the end of her shift. She sits in the front. She picks up the book from the dash.

Do you read, zero eight? she says, with a lilting interest in her tone.

Doesn't everybody? I've finished it anyway. D'you wanna borrow it?

'Sure.'

She puts it in her handbag.

'Thanks.'

Pulling up, I watch her walk to the flat, her mother's place, where she leaves her daughter. She's on her own, it must be hard. She has her hair pulled back in a ponytail, carries herself upright. I glanced at her profile while we were stopped at the lights. The bags under her eyes are defined very lightly, like a ridge of soft-blown sand. These days, this is the kind of detail that makes me fall in love. When I was younger, any female interest at all would do it. But now, if there's anything even slightly off, like a wrong-shaped ear-lobe, that's it, it's no good. I glanced at her again as the lights changed. Her ear-lobes were not the wrong shape.

Can this really be happening? I pass by the station in the early evening now and pick her up, on her way in. I'm a cab driver, I've got an excuse for driving around.

He picked me up beside the station the first time. I was walking from Mum's after dropping Alison off. I was noticing something curious. There are some punks that hang about in the buffet playing pinball. They're always there, this constant, in my life, almost comforting. That night, the punks weren't in. He took me by surprise, stopping hard by the kerb. He drives this old blue Merc. He'd already got the window wound down. D'you fancy being poached? he said. Poaching is picking up fares off the street. They're not supposed to do that, minicabs. I'd been having an off day. I was thinking about Me and Jim. I don't miss Jim any more, I really don't. Everyone gets moody sometimes.

Thanks, I said, and lowered myself into the passenger seat.

◆ ❖ ◆

One late Wednesday, there's only me on the plot. They've all gone, the rest. It's not worth their while hanging around. I'm just making my way back to base, thinking I might take in some beer, talk for a while, when she radios me.

'Zero eight, do you read?'

– Roger I do. Did you finish the book?

'Very droll, zero eight [that was the kind of impact I was looking for]. Can you make your way to 22 Summerbank? I've got an airport waiting for you there. Over.'

– Roger, I sigh. What d'you reckon?

'Sorry?'

– The book.

'Good. He's a nervous wreck, isn't he.'

There was no question in her voice, she just said it like a fact.

– Who? I said, Holden? Over.

'Roger.'

– I never thought about it like that. I thought it was funny mostly. Over.

'People pick things up in different ways, zero eight.'

– Different what? There was a crackle in the air. Come again, you're breaking up.

'I said I think it's a matter of interpretation, zero eight. Did you catch that?'

– Yeah . . . Roger.

I parked up, went to get my fare, still thinking. She was smart. I didn't know how I stood with her, to tell you the truth. Summerbank is a tower block. The passenger was an elderly man. I helped him down the stairs with his suitcases. I helped him into the back, he was a bit frail. I clunked the door behind him and moved the car off slow. I mean, I was in love with her alright.

I give the POB.

'Roger, rog.' Her voice is languid, and I picture her leaning back in her chair smoking, the wisps curling over those dunes beneath her eyes.

'Your controller is female?' The old man speaks in an accent, East European.

Uh-uh.

His question seems to be loaded. I don't know what he means. I don't follow him up though.

Where are you flying to? I ask instead.

'Ukraine.'

That's part of Russia?

'No more. We have our independence now.'

Are you going for a holiday?

'No, my boy, I'm going home.'

What's Ukraine like? It's an idiot question, but he's an

unusual fare and I feel like talking. It keeps me awake for one thing.

'Where I come from, we have great caviar and champagne. Cheap.'

Oh yeah, I think. Sure. It doesn't sound like the pictures I've seen on the TV, food queues and so on. I play him along though.

Sounds good.

'Sure it's good. And the girls . . .'

He trails off, laughing gently, like the girls must be fabulous.

On the return I'm thinking more about the Ukrainian than her. I'm feeling light-headed with tiredness as usual, I'm thinking about Russia, the Kremlin, Snow. I feel like Russia would be cold, but the man, the old man, he was warm. It's late. It's that kind of thought.

Near to base, I pick up the cans. When I arrive at the office, zero three's in there. They're chatting. I don't think it was anything too intimate, but I feel jealous. I thought it would be just me and her. I thought everyone else had gone. I hand the beers round anyway. Zero three knocks his back, crushes the can, tosses it into the wastebox, and leaves straight off.

'Bye. I'm whacked.'

Excellent. I thought he'd hang around just to piss me off. I sit on the filing cabinet beside her, sipping, and then she starts talking, slowly and distantly, her dress tucked under her feet and she tells me this story about Jim and her and the baby. When she finishes, I want to kiss her, but I don't think she'd welcome it. I really don't.

Oh, sorry, I forgot, she says, Mandy called when you were at the airport. She said could you pick up some Calpol from the all-night garage on your way home? Jamie's a bit off.

He's alright?

'Yeah, nothing too serious, she just said he was a bit off.'

I guess I'd better go.

'Roger.'

When I'm nearing home, her voice comes over the air.

'Zero eight. Zero eight.'

– Yeah. I'm receiving you.

'Catch you later?'

– What d'you mean? D'you mean you'd like to?

'Roger . . . Yeah. I mean I'd like to.'

'Zero eight, are you still there? Over.'

– Yeah, roger. I'd like to too. Catch you later, I mean. Yeah.

She's told me something.

Don't ever tell anybody anything.

I look out at the stars. I'm thinking. Maybe you shouldn't ever listen to people either, I'm thinking. Maybe you shouldn't ever listen to people either.

Upstairs, Jamie's sweating more than usual. It's a fever, Mandy says, spooning the medicine into his mouth while I hold him in the crook of my arm, stroking his brow with my hand. I lay him onto the white sheet, and pull the covers up to his neck, kissing him on each cheek. Just like the old man did to me at the airport, after he'd handed over the money – he leant forward and kissed me on both cheeks. It was odd, like a benediction. I sit down on the bed, turning the ignition key over and over in my hand.

Swimming

I drive in through the thin suburban fringe of Telford. I think about the woman from this morning. She looked at me oddly when I made my request. Sitting stout in her glass cubicle, she paused and weighed me up between the odd look and speaking. I put on my innocent-little-boy smile.

'No. You can't photograph when the public are in.'

I shifted the smile to my disappointed look.

'Come back at eight in the morning. I'll be opening up, but no one will be here until nine. You can do it then.'

I offered her my full-beam smile and thanked her, saying I'd see her then, then. Her expression remained blank. Something about her made me think of East Germany.

I concentrate on driving. I'm being filtered onto the ring road. I'm always being filtered onto a ring road. On the radio, the football fans' phone-in is coming to an end. The part-time politician who hosts it is winding the affair up.

'So it's goodbye from me until next week, when once again I'll be able to share in more soccer chat with you – the people who really matter. The fans.'

Sure thing, Rotund One. Nothing I like more than listening to some fat sleaze condescend to the people who really matter. Especially one who calls football Soccer.

I've stayed with this programme for the whole of the drive. Aside from the annoyance factor, there's been a bonus feature. The boys in the newsroom have been interrupting with updates on a hostage-taking situation that's happening in an Indian restaurant in downtown central Telford. I congratulate myself on my timing. I come here maybe once a year, and I'm going to catch the big one this very night. I hope it's still going on when I get there. I get very excited when I see blue and white cordon tape and silently-orbiting siren lights. The fat sleaze has gone, replaced by country music. I push in the tape. It's my girlfriend's car, so it's my girlfriend's tape, so it's Leonard Cohen. Leonard sings:

> Give me crack, anal sex, take the only tree that's left,
> Stuff it up the hole in your culture.
> Give me absolute control over every living soul,
> I've seen the future brother. It is murder.

I like this song. It rocks along. I like Leonard in upbeat form.

Things are still in full swing as we approach the incident. Me and Leonard, we slow right down as we pass the scene. I lower the window and ask a policeman on traffic redirection duty what on earth is going on. I can't help it. If I ever get the chance to be disingenuous with a copper, I take it.

'There's an armed man in the restaurant, Sir. Can you follow the traffic that way, please?'

An armed man? Really? I lean out of the window, eyebrows as high as I can get them.

'Yes, Sir. Sign of the times, I'm afraid. That way please.'

Two Sirs and a bit of social comment. It's always worth it.

Because of the diversion I get lost. Twice. Up some hills that I know I don't know. In and out of a housing estate. Past Siege Restaurant once more. I submit to the inevitable and ask some pedestrians. The pedestrians are not too sure, pedestrians are seldom sure, but they think it's back the way I've come from. It's usually back the way I've come from. I retrace my route, get somewhere near then ask again, this time a bloke on a bike. I've selected him with care. His cycling posture is stiffly upright. As we stop at the lights, he leans in through the window and I study his neatly-clipped moustache and dry complexion. He issues instructions with military precision, delivered with slight disdain. People should know where they're going. Five minutes later I pull up outside Stevens's.

Stevens's thirtieth. The reason I'm here. To meet up with this particular collection of old pals. Each year I select one event like this from the dwindling number. Most of the weddings are over now, divorce parties yet to begin. Landmark birthdays it is. I still like Stevens. I've even got him a present. I'm early because of tomorrow. I walk down to the pub before I commit myself to the party. Dave Fields is in there with his wife. I don't recognize her. I think the only time I've met her was at the wedding. No one could be expected to reconcile a once-seen bride with the same person sorting out a Silk Cut down the pub. Dave and I greet each other warmly. He calls me Hewitt, I call him Fields. It looks good, but we're on the fringe of each other's circles and I barely know him. Mrs Fields and I kiss each other on the cheek dispassionately. There's a band in the pub, moving black boxes around, setting up equipment. When the amps and drums are in place it's going to be a tight, loud squeeze. The band are called Jasper and the Last Boys. I drink a quick, warm pint of mild, make small talk with the Fieldses whilst admiring the band's outfits. The small talk is minuscule. I move swiftly on to the party.

'Hi, Hewitt, you fucker.'

Happy Birthday Stevens.

To a chorusette of Hi, Hewitt, you fucker, I respond with my Hi, Gilligham, Matt, Tim. Robbins! Cat, Man. Hello, Mitchell, you ugly bastard.

The atmosphere is warm and smoky. Punch, vodka jelly, spliffs. Part of the brief I give myself in checking this lot out is the monitoring of abuse levels, drug habits, beer guts. I'm a bit vicarious about it all now. I can't be arsed. I feel too unwell the next day, to be honest. I'm a light-weight. Mitchell brings his roundly-glowing kisser close up.

'Hewitt, where were you in Amsterdam, eh? You fuck-ing lightweight.'

I was with you most of the time. Shitface.

I stare through the shiny surface of his eyes as he attempts to sort out whether this is a truth or not, tries to find a memory somewhere deeper in. I can see he's strug-gling. He gives up, changes tack.

'Stevens says you're only staying for a bit. That right?'

Yeah.

'What are you on about? You're here now. You're in for the night, mate.'

No. Sorry. I've got to go and take some photos at eight in the morning.

Mitchell wrinkles, frowns, furrows. It's too much for him, this idea, it smells deviant.

'What for?'

Cos I want to. There's no one in the pool then; it's the only time I can do them. I've arranged it with the woman.

'You're photographing a swimming pool?'

Yeah.

'Why?'

It's old. Victorian. Used to swim there when I was a kid. It's a bit moody. Not many of them left.

I think I've given him a reasonable tranche of explanations here. Something for him to ponder.

'You're a fucking weirdo, Hewitt.'

That's me, Mitchell. I'm a fucking weirdo. By the way, if you ever want to know anything about crack or anal sex, Mitchell's your man.

Returning to the car, I roll a cigarette before pulling off. I should be back in time for Match of the Day. I've had a couple of beers and a coffee. Model Citizen. As I enjoy the flickering of the overhead lights, speeding up with the motion, I run the alternative through my mind. I could have gone the distance and driven back to Stoke first thing. This is how it would have gone: following a brief alcohol-induced coma, I'd have woken fully-clothed, stinking, needing a gallon of juice and Paracetamols as a matter of urgency. I'd have been able to find neither. Atavistically, I'd have lit up, coughing horribly. My eyes would be open by now, but little able to see. If I was lucky, I wouldn't be able to remember trying to have sex with someone I'd known for years and never fancied anyway. If I was especially lucky that would be because the coma arrived before I tried it. I'd step over snuffling bodies on the way out. I'd be sweating beer on the drive back. And then I'd have to try to work the camera. I know I've made the right move. I turn Leonard back on:

> *Everybody knows you love me baby, everybody knows you really do.*
> *Everybody knows that you've been faithful, give or take a night or two.*

Sardonic lyric, simple rhyme, groovy tune. I like Leonard. He's a poet. I get back in time for Match of the Day.

At seven-thirty on a Sunday morning I feel like the only person in the world who's awake. But I like driving at this time of day. Deserted streets, silence as silent as a city ever gets. I think of people snoring in their beds. I think of people sweating out last night's beer. I think of being held hostage in an armed siege in an Indian restaurant. It wouldn't be nice, would it? Poppadums, bhajis and bullets. I'd be staring at the wallpaper, me, thinking, Is this how I'm gonna end my days, splattered over flock-fucking-wallpaper? I'd be thinking interior design. It wouldn't be cheering me up.

◆

Across the road I notice an old man leaving a newsagent's with his paper rolled under his arm. It's still before eight. They get up early, old people, don't they? Catching time while they've still got it. The newsagent's is the last building standing in a bloody great wasted flatland. Every time I pass through here, there's less structure than there was the time before. You'd need a big tree to plug the hole in this culture, Leonard my old son. You'd need to reforest.

I stop outside a building which, for the first time, I notice is called the Queen Victoria Jubilee Building. And I remember suddenly, from nowhere, the Jubilee celebrations for Our Queen. Union Jacks and jam tarts and little waifs on the nick. I'd rather stay in. Or I'd rather have gone swimming. This was my pool. Tunstall Baths is what it's really called. Across the road there used to be a bus rank, six shelters made of green corrugated iron and broken glass. You could harbour there while waiting for the bus to come, to take you to places which, now I try the names out in my head, sound frankly odd. Fegg Hayes, Sneyd Green, Chell Heath, Brindley Ford and Brown Edge. Brown Edge? Who would want to go to a place called Brown Edge? Anyway, you can't go there from here any more because the bus shelters have all gone.

I gather up the camera and tripod and walk into the foyer. The smell. Chlorine naturally, but also bleach, wet towel, sweat. And shampoo and soap. The sound. It echoes around, bouncing off water and ceramic to whisper away, losing itself in the air above, air which has a saturated quality, so that just for a moment it's difficult to breathe in quite the usual way. Your body goes tic, tic, tic, making adjustments to take in the O^2 in moist form. I'm not sure this happens in modern Leisure Pools. Air-conditioning systems probably keep the humidity level at some pre-determined ambient point. A computer where the pump room should be orchestrates a series of wave machines, geysers, rapids, waterfalls, jet-sprays, fountains, a laser light-show and a disco soundtrack. But can you put in a few lengths? Not a hope. Something's going to get you. And another thing: the water will be hot. I don't want a bath or an interactive experience, I want a swim.

What I have in front of me as I nudge through the double doors is what a swimming pool should be. A twenty-five by twelve-yard rectangle, three feet deep at the shallow end and six feet deep at the deep end. Along each length a regular sequence of identical doors with opaque glass panels in the top quarter. Behind them, tiny changing cubicles. At each corner of the deep end, open shower blocks with big chrome taps, industrial heads and red ter-racotta floor-tiles embossed with the pattern of a Lincoln biscuit. Overhead, structural ironwork supports the glazed roof. Light floods the water, which shimmers and shines. This is what a swimming pool should be.

I stand still for a moment. I don't think I've been here for about fifteen years. Curiously, it doesn't appear smaller. Apart from a green plastic turtle a little below balcony level on the deep-end wall, it's just as I remember it. As fantastically austere as I had hoped. I step over the nasty footbath containing, it seems, the same orange disinfectant from years ago, and turn hard right to the steep steps which rise to the balcony. I have to go up there first. This was the vantage point and team base for school swimming galas. The thick mahogany handrail, buttressed by rudder-shaped supports, gleams in bitter-chocolate brown. The rails on which it rides glint sunlight off their glossy green paintwork. A single utilitarian plank running between the rail and the wall serves as seating. At the back, against the wall, there's a plinth from which standing spectators can view races. As I look down into the dead-still water, I can hear the cheering and whooping you get when a race is on. I can see myself aged about twelve, or maybe eleven. I'm clenching the chrome rail at the deep end, feet braced against the wall, waiting for the start of the twenty-five-yard backstroke. I'm wearing some rather natty red trunks, decorated with proficiency and distance badges sewn on by my mum. My stomach is knotted and contains butterflies. Come on. Come On.

On your marks, set, bang. You get a great echo from a pistol in here, but I don't hear it as my head flies back into the water. Whrrr. My arms are going like, well, someone whose arms are going really fast. It's no good though, there's an astonishingly rapid kid from Stanfields in the end lane. He's going to win by about half a pool. I'm going to come last. Then I'm going to have to return to this balcony, trying to hide my tears and pretending it means nothing to me. I'm not going to carry this off with any measure of success. In fact, I'm going to have to pretend I've picked up a cold down there, with the amount of snivelling that's going to be leaking from under the towel wrapped around my head. And my mates are not going to offer me any comfort. For this lot, a loser is someone to taunt. They know a lot about losers. They see them everywhere. They know a lot about taunting. It's standard conversation. I know. I've been round their houses. We get less of this at my house; my dad's not in much. That's why my mates like to stay round ours. I shift my stare from the water, unzip the bag, start sorting out the camera equipment.

Right back in the far corner I can capture almost the whole pool. A sexy perspective. Sex. I remember trying to grab a handful of Josephine Allen's bottom down there on a Saturday morning. She was an athlete and could deliver a prize-winning slap to the cheek. It was a trophy, a sort of badge of honour, to have your face stinging red from one of her anointments. Saturday mornings in a pool. Another world. Not home, not school, not the cinema, not the park. And not dry land. Remember all that excitement, emerging shivering in your trunks, trying it out with a big toe, testing the temperature? Someone pushes you from behind, and there you go, slithering and half-spinning in the air, engulfed, submerged, the air taken right out of you. Surfacing, you splutter, gurgle, choke, spit water. You try to grab the perpetrator by his ankle, he steps back – onto the outstretched arms of another someone who shoves him in. The fight continues in superb style. You can dive underwater and pull his trunks down, or leap on top of him, your hands splayed and linked and push his head under. You can engage in elaborately stagey group battles, each throwing the other through the air to come crashing back to a spectacularly safe landing. You can take a mouthful of water and spit it as high as you can get it, or straight into Nigel Gilligham's face. You've no regard for hygiene. Plenty of people have relieved themselves in there today. But it's brilliant, as near as you'll get to being on the moon. The age of innocence. When young hearts ran free. When landings were spectacularly safe.

I move downstairs and set up beside the edge. I go for a long shot down the length. Once, when I stood here, I was waiting for a change-over in the four-by-four one-hundred-yard freestyle relay. I was taking the third leg. Kevin Cooper was coming towards me. He was taking the second leg and was in second place. It's difficult, a change-over in a swimming relay. You watch your man coming nearer and nearer and you increase an already high rate of teetering. One false teeter and you're disqualified. But you need the tension, need to keep it tight, keep coiled, because you want maximum momentum as you dive. With a good dive you can cover over a quarter of a length. I remember that Kevin Cooper change-over. I got it dead right, made up all the ground on my leg and the fourth man took the victory. The four-by-four one-hundred-yard relay. That was more like it. What was I doing in the backstroke in the first place?

Cooper and I, we raced back to the balcony, wet bodies slithering off each other as we scuffled about. Then Josephine Allen got all flirty with him, the little git. The last time I saw him was through the window of a car I was driving a few years ago. He looked like one of those men I used to notice making for the Workingmen's Club in High Lane early in the evening on a Friday. He had side-boards, and I mean big sideboards, not cool ones. Double chin. Complexion like cowhide. Fat too, and never going to get any thinner. Oh yeah, I slowed right down and took it all in. I'd been reading a novel by one of the neo-skinhead school of writers at the time. I recalled a line from it that went: *And meanwhile time goes about its immemorial business of making everyone look and feel like shit. You got that? And meanwhile time goes about its immemorial business of making everyone look and feel like shit.*

I gaze down into the pool. Sometimes, when I stare into still water, I get an image of someone slowly drowning. It's never anyone in particular. And they're not thrashing about any more, they're already dead. The part I concentrate on is the hair, always the hair, eddying serenely about the face, still rippling as the body comes to rest on the bottom. It doesn't happen very often. And it has to be deep water.

Moving to the side of the pool, I focus across to the doors of the changing cubicles, their symmetrical reflections moving ever so slightly below. Thinking of Kevin Cooper has me thinking of Mark McVie. McVie never used to come swimming. At school he always feigned illness at the appropriate moment. We three used to play together in the evening. McVie liked to spice things up by introducing a criminal element. Riding your bike without lights, being

rude to adults. Planning heists on church roofs and building sites for lead. That sort of thing. We were on both sides
of the law though, attempting to apprehend villains as
well as trying to be them. We used to ride our bikes
through a long dark tunnel near Bath Pool Park, calling
out, Panther, Panther, where are you? frightened by our
own echoes. We were nearer than we knew. The Black Panther had kidnapped an heiress who was eventually found
hanging down a mineshaft about a mile from the area in
which we were making our enquiries.

One night McVie led us to a shop, he had a secret he
wanted to show us. The shop was on a corner near a pub.
There was a derelict flat above, McVie had found a way
into it. From there you could get into the shop, through a
loft-hatch between the shop and the derelict flat. He
wanted us all to go in, steal fags, sweets, porno mags, bat-
teries, to sell at school. I wouldn't do it. He and Kevin
Cooper sneered at me as they went off alone. The moment
of fissure. If you don't dare, you're out. I watched, from a
guarded distance, as they did business in the playground.
I only watched this once though, because the next time
they went back, the owner and the police were waiting for
them. I think it was six months they each got in Borstal.
They weren't out of school for so long because they were
sent inside during the long summer holiday between
Middle and High School. Neither of them ever spoke to
me much after that. McVie did once tell me about the
guards throwing medicine balls at their heads. At High
School I was in Form G, they were in Form S. A ripple
breaks across the surface of the water. At the far end a life-

guard has turned up and is introducing one of those long plastic ropes into the pool to divide the lanes up.

The stillness broken, I begin to pack the camera equipment away. I remember I often used to come back to the pool at the end of a session just to see the water quiet and unmoving, the surface stilled. I circuit the perimeter once and find myself smiling. It's nearly nine. Time to go. I bid farewell to the East German, a specialist in blank looks.

Outside, kids line up, dayglo plastic inflatables spilling out of shoulder bags. I'm glad to have got these shots. I've no idea why. I mean, I'm not doing a project or anything. I drive back towards my mum's house. Then I detour, taking a route I often use when I'm in town. I drive up a steep hill called Greenbank Road and turn left at the top. I slide the tape back in. As I slow down while I pass a house in which I once lived, Leonard sings:

> *I'm sentimental if you know what I mean;*
> *I love the country but I can't stand the scene.*

I don't catch the following line because the building which should be appearing next on my left-hand side doesn't. They've knocked down my old school. I can't believe it.

We turn a corner which should be in the shadow of the main building, a building which, externally, looked much like the swimming pool, and we park up. Beside me is a sign which reads, Demolition. Keep out. It's painted on one of the last pieces of remaining wall. Keep Out? You're joking, aren't you? There's bloody nothing left. I'm stunned. I used to love this school. They did great school dinners. This is Theft. I always pass by here. I do it deliberately. Kneeling now, I pick up a dusty red brick with a moulding on the face. It would have been from high up, one of the decorative corbel stones. It's beautiful. I take it to the car, put it in the boot. There are a few shots left on the film. Might as well finish it off on this devastation before the place is covered in fucking McHomes. I crunch across the playground and set the camera on the tripod. Through the lens, a Sunday-morning kid in scuffed clothes comes into view. I straighten up. The first person I'm able to blame. Before he can give me a What are you doing Mister? I ask him in an accusatory manner:

Why did they knock the school down?

'It was too old.'

Where are you going to school now, then?

'Stanfields.'

I snort. I used to go to school here.

I used to go to school here. I say it proudly. His face is a picture of uninterest. He wanders off. I don't suppose he'd have given a shit that I swam for the school team either. Back in the car, I make straight for home. I push the tape back in. Come on then, Leonard, give me an ending. The old crooner won't fail me, I know it.

Things are gonna slide, slide in all directions.
Won't be nothing, won't be nothing, you can measure anymore.

Thank you.

Last

Roll past the Methodist Hall where I used to sing hymns when I was young, splash through the puddle at the bottom of the hill where the road won't drain. Right on the corner there's the door to the shop, black-framed glass. A bell rings as you push it open, your nostrils assailed. A long wait on the worn lino. You consider going back to the door to sound the bell again, but if you linger just to the end of your patience, footsteps will be heard falling slow and heavy from the back, along the passage which leads to the Workshop, as it's called. You wait, standing surrounded. Box-ends with rectangular labels confront you, crammed floor to ceiling so you can't see what supports them. There must be shelves. Browns, buffs and blacks, the cardboard colonnades kick up an intense vertigo of heel and buckle. On the glass counter, in the glass counter, to the sides, back and under the glass counter, mended shoes await collection. I suppose. Dust shrouds them, and most appear not to be paired, they could have been there for years. Lone, he closes in, his odour outflanking him, colliding with the overriding smell of stale foot and new and old leather. Pulling into shot, he removes fogged, heavy-rimmed glasses, wipes the sweat from his brow on his filthy-dirty vest, cleans the spectacles on the hem wide-hanging over his belly, balances them once more on his nose. Squints.

George's lad, is it?

Is he getting blind?

No, it's me.

Ah. Come for some tea?

Well, it is that time of day.

Follow him through. I don't know how black and dirty it can be anywhere in the world that could be as black and dirty as it is down here. Off the passage to the left is the room where he works, with tacks, hammer and last, a million more shoes all over the place. It has a window, but it can't have been cleaned since the Second World War because it's no lighter than if it didn't have one at all. Stop on the threshold, inhale. Rubber? Yes. The other part of the smell. Follow him upstairs to the living-room where he keeps it all. His kitchen, on a table by the window, a bit cleaner this one, but it's always November in here anyway. If it were summer you'd never know. Tea, Pot, Kettle, his spoons in a jar, and bread, white and uncut, and after he's got the tea things going he carves two big slices, skewers one on the fork, haunches in front of the fire and toasts. The best smell of toast. He gives me tea in a white metal mug with a thin blue rim. He's got honey for the toast, the thick kind, rising on the knife like wax but hard to spread. He passes a slice over, torn.

What have you been up to then?

Nothing much.

Just waiting to come down here.

The door goes three times while we take our break, but he isn't bothered.

They'll be back.

At the bottom of the mug he's left all the leaves like he used to. Never strains it. I've forgotten, as ever, and I spit the mouthful straight into the fire. Yuck.

They're good for you, you know. Make you mighty.

He swallows his, rests against the edge of the table, puts his mug down.

On the way out, he stumbles in front of me on the stair, semi-crash-lands, awkward, his bulk mashed into the corner.

Are you alright? And I try to help him up.

He straightens slow, panting. He doesn't say anything. Moves into the workshop, rests his hands on the cold inverted foot, stares ahead a long time. I just stand in the doorway, waiting and watching, until he remembers himself. He picks up a shoe, a workboot, fits it over the anvil, lifts the umber hammer from the burnt bench and begins tapping at the sole.

I move away, leave, and the bell rings.

Outside I press my face to the shop window, to see if he'll come, because I know he's forgotten about me, and the bell should have been a customer coming in, not me going out. But he doesn't come. And I knew he wouldn't.

Some Beach

Walking along, the boy trailing behind, the sky and the sea merged into one band of blankness. The grey breakers smashed the shore.

Though it was getting on for winter, I liked to take him down to the beach on my patrols. I told him the air would do him good. He'd complain, spend the time miserably kicking pebbles.

'The beach is boring.'

The air's good for you.

'Don't care.'

I'm a grown-up, so I'm right. And pull your scarf up.

I like to think I played the line with a certain irony but the boy wasn't into it. He was a little young for irony. And anyway, when anyone ever tried telling me what to do, ironically or otherwise, I never liked it. I appreciated the defiance in his face. But I was responsible for him, so he had to come.

We found a starfish, a small one, stiff, six sharp legs of orange-amber and tiny patterns of sea-Braille across its body, a dangerous invitation to touch.

What's that? asked the boy.

An echinoderm of the class Asteroidia.

'Oh.'

The light changed as a stray cloud passed the thin mid-day sun and right then, at exactly that moment, a jellyfish drifted in front of us, fat in translucent rubberiness with its miniature legs, useless, borrowed from a passing squid. Memories played of treading barefoot on one of these, in North Wales, and of some special cure being applied to the sting – vinegar? – at a campsite behind the beach. The sun returned and glinted through the clear body, just a thread of veiny tissue here and there to inform us of a presence. We stood regarding the menace.

'They sting, don't they?'

Yeah, they do. And their trick is that often you don't see them until it's too late.

Seagulls swirled overhead in their usual way. We sighted them along our forefingers, shooting them down.

Bang, you're dead.

The boy liked that. For a short time.

We stopped and sat on a large smooth rock with a dipped-in bit that made a seat, swinging our legs, bashing our ankles against the side, throwing small pebbles at a big pebble. We missed more than we hit.

Some days, even with the boy there beside me, I imagined I saw the two of them further along the beach, him with his mother. The surface rolling underfoot, I'd try to steady myself and quiet the tumbling and the noise. Everything seemed to be magnified. But the waves kept up their rhythm and other music drifted over from the arcade. I'd stare down the stretch and they'd be gone.

From the corner of my eye I noticed a crab watching us. I twisted to face the crustacean head-on, not exactly sure if that was the right way to face up to a crab.

What's your problem? I asked it.

The crab didn't move, just sat there, its beady black eyes sheening in an odd dead way. I shifted into performance.

Have you ever heard the joke about the prawn and the crab?

The crab twitched its big claw.

I took this as an indication to tell the joke.

A crab, a boy crab, meets a girl prawn. They get along Fabulously so they start courting. After a while, on a romantic moonlit evening, the crab gets down on one [I assessed the crab] pincer. He offers her a gift, an oyster pearl. 'Prawn,' says the crab, 'I love you and I want to marry you. I'm going to come round to your place tonight and ask your father for your hand.' 'Oh crab, I love you too,' the prawn says, 'but it will never work, my father won't allow it. He says that crabs are stupid and not to be trusted. And most of all he can't stand their ridiculous sideways walk.' 'Don't you worry about that,' says the crab. And that night he knocks on prawn's door. He walks down the hall in a dead straight line and shakes the hand of the prawn's father. 'Oh crab, how clever of you! You're walking straight!' whispers the prawn. 'Shh,' says the crab, 'I'm absolutely pissed!'

I could see the crab was laughing, enjoying this. I was

147

pleased to be able to understand crabs as creatures that can take a joke. If you ask me, this joke is the ideal one for the seaside visitor. Love always gets the landlocked to the coast. In the beginning there's a need to see somewhere brimful of magic, to catch a feeling like you feel inside. An urge to see something so big you can't explain it, space without an edge. The crab was looking expectant, like it was saying, Go on, tell us another. Sorry, I said, that's the only one I know.

Some nights we used to go skinny dipping. About a hundred yards off the shore a small rowing-boat danced around a buoy. We'd get drunk then swim out, climb in and try to make love, burning our skin on the coiled-up rope and tarpaulin, trying to make some kind of purchase on each other. In the morning we woke up tasting of salt, our bodies bruised. Later we'd go to a tiny cinema with makeshift seats, the projector so close behind that the noise of its whirring was louder than the soundtrack. The families around us, holidaying, taking it all in; she and I struggling to kill our giggles as Shelley Winters swam her underwater escape in The Poseidon Adventure. She was so naturally buoyant it was a miracle she could get submerged at all.

I must have been looking like I was far away.

What are you thinking about? asked the boy.

I wasn't thinking about anything. How about you?

'I asked first.'

He did. He asked first. He knew the answer I'd given him wasn't the truth. Me and the boy, we'd been drifting around like this for a while now. Since summer in

fact. Since she disappeared. We were on one long holiday, but to be honest we'd had enough of it. We
wouldn't find her out here. Watching the waves, that's
all we were doing.

Do you fancy a go on the dodgems, kid? I asked it in cod
American.

'I sure do, Pop.' He was good at the routine.

It was so end-of-season at the fair that more than half
the cars were banked up at one end, covered with canvas.
We took our seats in the orange one, it's always the
fastest. The guy took our money like he couldn't care less.
There was only one other couple riding. There was music
playing overhead:

Oohhwahhwahh. Oohhwahhwahh. Oohh.

Sweet Sensation. We liked that one.

The other couple, they were schoolkids, arms round
each other, love-bites lacing their necks. They kept
bumping us, and we kept bumping them back. They
started it. When the ride finished – it seemed to be an
extra long one – we got off, and I did a sideways walk to
amuse the boy.

'Are you drunk? Like the crab?'

Not any more. No.

He took hold of my hand.

Listen, kid. I reckon it's about time we quit this town.
How about you?

The love-bite lad ruffled the boy's hair on his way off the
track, and the love-bite girl gave him a miniature curly-

candy hockey-stick. Thanks, he said, unpeeling the cellophane wrapper, sucking on the hook.

'Sure thing, Pop, let's split.'